ON A
STRANGE
WORLD
RUNNING

ON A
STRANGE
WORLD
RUNNING

By: Malcolm Wayne Puckett, Ph.D.

Copyright Information

On a Strange World Running
By: Malcolm Wayne Puckett, Ph.D.
©2020 By: Malcolm Wayne Puckett, Ph.D.

Published by:
Good News Fellowship Ministries
220 Sleepy Creek Rd.
Macon, Georgia 31210

ISBN-13: 978-1-7344999-3-3

Most Scriptures used in this book are from the New International Version of the Bible.

Format and Cover Design by: Lisa Walters Buck

Contents

Acknowledgments

With immense pleasure, I give credit to those who helped me with this adventure we call "writing a book."

First, I thank my wife, Aimee Michelle, and my daughter, Natalie Renee, for their tolerance and help. My wife was gracious in giving me space to write. My daughter read the copyrighted version years ago and said,

"O, Daddy, this is good!"

That sure helped! She also gave feedback on the plot, most of which I incorporated.

Others who reviewed the manuscript include Stanley Mingo and Owen Keith Puckett. Their insight and comments were encouraging and helpful toward finishing this work.

For all who have sustained me through the years with your prayers and help, I ask God to bless you greatly and hope you enjoy this fruit which your love enabled me to produce.

Introduction

Have you ever felt completely alone? Maybe like no one understands you? No one cares? Then you will empathize with the main character of this book.

This book pulls together several of the feelings I have had in challenging times in my life. Often, I thought God had deserted me and left me to live each day in deep emotional pain for the rest of my days. And I often faced obstacles and foes who wished me harm. Eventually, the tough times would pass, and life would go on. Sometimes better and sometimes much better. Times of victory often followed these tough places.

When you read, I hope you will empathize with the main character. Share his feelings and thoughts. Then at the end, you will feel his mixed feelings of triumph tempered with sadness. As I wrote, I laughed and cried and felt with him. I hope you do too.

You are about to go on a trip of forced self-discovery, confrontations with relentless enemies, and stretched faith. Bon voyage!

- Malcolm Wayne Puckett, March 2020

SECTION I
Who Am I?

Chapter 1: Day One – Escape!

I need to get out of here! I carefully ran from shadow to shadow, avoiding anyone who might be around to catch a glimpse of me. *There is an alley! Maybe it goes to the wall.*

With a quick look for peering eyes, I ran to the alley and headed in the direction of the outside wall. My emotions were hot with fear and anger, so my legs and arms were flailing the air. If I could fly, I would have. I then saw the wall ahead of me. I looked left and right along the wall while I ran. *There is a door in the wall!*

I ran to it, seeing it had a heavy cross bar. Heaving off the cross bar and tossing it aside, I pushed hard at the old wooden door. Nothing. I stepped back and rammed my shoulder against it. It absorbed my thrust with a muffled thud, still not moving.

Gasping for breath, my shoulder throbbing, I stumbled back and looked closely at it. The hinges were not on this side, but the cross bar was. *Who has the hinges on the outside of a city wall?* I picked up the cross bar and used it to ram against the door again. This time it gave a little. I kept ramming it until I could see some daylight. Tossing the cross bar away, I leaned into the door and shoved with all my strength. This time it opened a little more, so I shoved at it again. Slowly it pushed open more with each shove.

I saw grass and trees and kept on shoving. Glancing down, I could see the door was scraping an arc in the grass and sod as it moved.

Contrasted with my dark fear of what was behind me, a sunlit grassy field with a few rocks next to the wall lay before me. I opened it enough to step quickly through and look sharply around as my eyes adjusted to the light.

Out from the wall was a forest nearly a hundred yards away, and its edge ran parallel to the wall. Hurriedly I shoved the door shut and begin to run, but then I saw a rather large rock and stopped. I suddenly noticed that I was carrying some bags (*What? I have bags!*), so I dropped them and rolled the rock back to the door, leaning the rock against it. As extra barricading, I quickly used the side of my foot to scrape some of the sod against the door and around the rock.

Muffled sounds of feet running on the pavement came from inside, so I grabbed my baggage in a new rush of fear and sprinted to the forest directly in front of me. As I crashed gasping into the underbrush, I heard the guards behind me start to pound on the door. *They must have seen the cross bar off the door.* Hiding my things under some small bushes between two trees about ten yards into the wood, I crouched down and looked back.

The door cracked open in the high wall. The crack grew wider, and one guard stepped out and moved the rock. Then the door opened wide as the rest of the group of six stepped out into the sunlight. They came through and hesitated, looking in all directions and talking all at once. The leader gathered them around and quickly discussed their approach. They split up into three pairs, one set headed left along the edge of the forest, another headed right. The last pair walked directly toward me. The others jogged off and were soon out of earshot.

The two closest to me began walking quickly toward the path in the woods which passed about 15 feet to my left. I hurriedly considered what to do. *I feel I have fighting skills. Should I jump them, or should I let them go by? Would the martial arts of Earth work on these creatures? Do they have similar pressure points? They have similar bodies to humans, only slightly taller and thinner. Also, they have swords, and I don't know what I have or how to reach them, so I must be very sure before attacking them, even in surprise.*

My natural urge was to run in the panic I felt, and I thought I might be faster than they were, but probably not when carrying the baggage. The backpack was exceptionally large and heavy. Also, running would give me away and enable them to follow my trail. Options of my training and experience flashed through my excited mind. Now that my breathing was quieter and steadier, I decided to try a surprise attack on the guards if they came too close to me.

They paused at the forest edge and looked into the shadows. I knew they didn't hear me. I recognized them as young and small guards compared to the rest. Their leader must have thought I would not have gone straight into the trees, and so he sent the youngest here just to be sure. Also, he might have thought I came out of the door several minutes ago and would be well ahead of them.

With a slight look of fear on their faces they walked the few yards to my left into the shaded world before them. Instinctively, I knew they were too scared to see me if I was careful. I decided not to attack but follow them for a while. Yet I wondered why armed guards would show fear of one single person such as me.

They passed me and continued to look ahead. When they were safely beyond me, I felt calm enough to look around at my surroundings under foot to see what would affect my trailing them. Seeing only small bushes and grasses with no thorns or dry leaves, I began to follow along the little trail, occasionally hiding off to the side when they might be able to catch a glimpse of me.

As I walked, I noticed the details of the forest. So many physical features of this planet reminded me of Earth. This could have been a forest in the Appalachian Mountains in America with taller trees and softer bushes. The trees looked like a cross between southern pine and hardwood trees. The leaves which had fallen retained some moisture and did not rustle like leaves of Earth. The small bushes and grasses along the path were frail and thin, offering little resistance to my shoes. I spotted an occasional cluster of small trees here and there among the taller trees, but not along the path itself. Following the young guards was easier than back home because of this. The bushes and leaves made almost no sound as I moved.

After a brisk pace for nearly an hour, I had trailed them through several alternating thick patches and then openings in the wood. There the sunlight beamed down in lovely rays through the tops of these slender trees over 100 feet tall. The guards were slowing down and acted more relaxed. They stopped, and one pulled out a handmade horn and blew several melodious blasts, some long and some short. I assumed he was alerting others in the area, reaching even back to the city. After a few brief words between them, they turned to go back to the city.

I felt a new rush of the flight urge as they came back my way. Quickly I hid my baggage behind a bush, then I hid myself off to the side of the path farther into the wood. *Should I try to subdue them now and take their weapons? No, not yet.* There were too many unknowns, and no one had discovered me for now. I was still feeling an intense sense of fear and confusion and was not sure if my actions would be smooth enough to prevail over both of these taller creatures.

Though still on high alert emotionally, I could not help but admire their slender frames over six feet tall and the smoothness of their medium brown skin as they passed by. The human-like faces looked serious, contrasted with their light brown hair which draped wistfully down to the napes of their necks. Each face was without hair, except for eyebrows. What beautiful creatures these were! Why was I so afraid of them? I almost wanted to walk out and talk to them, but I dare not. I found them to be much like humans on Earth, yet their handsomeness was far beyond what I know there.

For uniforms, each had a silver shirt and pants with wide ice-blue belt. Over this, he wore a jacket of light unwrinkled material which had sleeves to the elbows and was open about a foot wide in the front. The jacket reached down to just above the knees. It was silver with an ice-blue border on both sides of the front going up and around the neck. He carried a four-foot sword in a sheath at his waist.

There was an air of nobility and grace about them. It was like looking at ancient Roman or Greek gods, or angels in the descriptions in the Bible. Yet I did not know whether they were benevolent or malicious.

After they were well past me, I paused to let my emotions finally dial down. Sweat poured off my brow, the sweat of heat which is within. My hands were shaking, and my breathing had been quick and shallow, but soon I was composed enough to gather my things and look farther into the wood.

It appeared to be about noon, so I had a few hours before dark. I set off at a brisk pace away from the city to put as much distance between it and me as possible. After a while I had to find a place to spend the night, and maybe try to remember the events which led me to this lonely flight. *No time to entertain fear or feel sorry for myself now. I must prepare.* Night would come, and I was alone with unknown items in my baggage. *Shelter, then food, then rest.*

Many a tree and bush passed me by as I walked briskly along the small and winding path. After a few miles along the trail, I aimed my way off the path to further isolate myself from anyone searching later. I hurried along while noticing birds and small creatures playing among the trees. Most seemed unafraid of me, and they were too small to be any threat to my safety. There were no signs of larger creatures along the way.

Marching through the wood long enough to begin feeling physically tired, I saw a large hill up ahead to the right of the direction I was taking. As I came closer, I noticed the trees and underbrush covered parts of it well. As I walked around and explored it, I found it had rock outcroppings farther up. Climbing up the sides, I found one spot was remarkably similar to a small cave with a soft sandy floor, certainly with enough overhang for shelter from rain. It was also tight and deep enough to protect from large animals. (At this point, I knew almost nothing about the weather and only of the animals I had seen on my walk.) A flint like rock as large as a plate made a good scraping tool to prepare the spot as a bed and windbreak, so I got to work on the floor of my new home.

After a short while I finished and sat down in my new place to rest. The view allowed me to see over some of the trees for several miles. No trees were directly in front of the shelter, so I would be able to see any large creatures or humanoids approaching. Some small bushes lined the opening, so the shelter was hidden until anyone came close to it.

A voice inside said I had forgotten something, something particularly important. But I did not want to think about it now. The suppressed feelings were strong and demanding, but I pushed them down for a while longer. Dealing with them right then would only have distracted me from what was most needful. Why that was true I did not know. I just needed to keep pressing on.

Then I felt I needed to see what I had on me before I had any more encounters. I found a large hunting knife toward the back left on my belt. *How did I miss this?* I also had keys and other small items that would not be as helpful, although they indicated something about my personality.

Thirst and hunger came to save me from my thoughts about the personal items, so I got up after a few minutes of gazing at the restful scene to look for food and water. I still felt afraid, but having a shelter, even for one night, gave some comfort. A stream nearby provided some amazingly fresh water that looked as clear as any mountain stream on Earth. I found out later that most of the water on this world comes from artesian springs.

Some smaller trees nearby had purple fruits shaped like pears which looked good to eat, so I picked some of them off the lower branches. Right now, I could not be concerned about whether they were good for food or not. My hunger and thirst drove me to take the risk.

For the first few bites, I ate carefully and slowly. When I felt all right, I started eating like a man in a hurry, stuffing the fruit into my mouth and eating feverishly. With significant effort, I made myself slow down and enjoy the food. These "pears" were very moist and had a rich and full taste, more like ripe plums. After eating three and tossing away the hard pits at the core, the feverish desire settled down.

Feeling calmer, I remembered while following the guards that some of the bushes we passed were bearing berries I might be able to eat. Searching for a few minutes revealed some of these bushes under a dense area of the tall trees. I picked a shirt full of berries which resembled raspberries, then noticed a tree with some different fruit a little farther away. Two bunches of fruit which looked like clusters of small apples hung low enough for me to pluck, so I returned to the shelter with what I told myself was a full-course meal. As I walked, I ate from my shirt collection, nearly finishing before I reached the shelter. The additional foods were also quite moist and satisfied the rest of my thirst as well. My hands cleaned easily in the soft grasses all around.

At this point the physical and emotional strain of the day began to weigh upon me. Darkness approached. Fatigue from fear, walking for hours, and hunting for shelter and food had left me exhausted. Too tired to process that day's events, I lay down where I could awaken to protect myself if necessary. I marveled at the twin suns setting straight out from me and quickly fell asleep. After a few stirrings at strange sounds, I soon rested for the night.

Chapter 2: Day Two - Fight to Survive

In the morning, I awoke with a start. I forgot where I was. After a few tense moments of raw fear, the events of the day before flashed through my mind, and I began to calm down. Dawn had been past for a little while. Birds were singing strange songs, and small animals were chattering.

Unhappy to realize it was NOT just a bad dream, I lay back down for a spell and stretched. Hunger and thirst overwhelmed my disappointment, and I did not want to analyze my situation just yet, so I decided to get up. Stiff muscles needed a couple of minutes to loosen up, then I ventured out to eat some more of the fruit on the nearby trees. The berries served as dessert.

The scenery was beautiful in the morning, with all the plants and features of the land at sharper and taller angles than on Earth. After I looked around while eating, I decided to explore this part of the world a little. I adjusted my shoes, stretched a little, and set out for a walk.

My anxiety was much less than I expected. It felt comfortable there. The land with its plants and animals seemed to flow with peace like a wide river flows with water.

The landscape here was of rolling forested hills with occasional open grassy places. The open places were either fields with tall grass and small bushes or hills with rocky ravines and outcroppings of rock with a stream or creek at times. One cliff sported a tiny waterfall which extended like a graceful diver into a clear pool below. I climbed over rocks along the bottom of the cliff to get near the pool. A few berries of a new kind made a rich snack as I sat beside the beautiful display of sight and sound.

A melancholy mood washed over me. Here I was alone and surrounded by nature's beauty on a strange world. I felt alone and yet not alone. The mystery of my feelings was inscrutable, so I moved on.

As I began to round a tight grove of trees, I felt a sharp impulse to stop and look carefully about. I crouched down quickly and peered through the grassy growth at the base of a tree. Looking all around, I found my trained senses had served me well. Two soldiers were walking through the forest about 500 feet away.

These were the same type of creatures as what I had evaded back at the city, yet not like them. They were of similar height with different uniform and bearing. Their skin was like the others but with very white hair. Where the others had silver and ice blue on the uniforms, these had gold and crimson, respectively.

These two had a sinister look and feel to them. The earlier creatures seemed fluid and relaxed in their gait. These two acted like they were in deadly earnest and walked at a stiff, stilted pace. They were peering all around into the forest, occasionally stopping to listen to the sounds. *They must be looking for me!*

Approaching the base of my hill, they spoke curtly to one another and split up. One went to the right around the other side of the hill, and the other came toward me. I would have liked to run off, but he was too close, and the underbrush here was so short he would surely see me anyway. I stayed down and found a better place to hide off to the side behind a wide tree.

He was walking in a line which would lead him right past my tree. Every step brought him closer and put me more on edge. I prepared mentally for defending myself if discovered, hoping all the time he would miss me. As he got closer still, I caught a glimpse of his face. This was a face which had witnessed much cruelty, probably by his own hands.

Suddenly, he caught a glimpse of me as he passed the tree. He backed away slightly and pulled his long slender sword, then turned it swiftly around and swung at me. I jumped up and to the right, so he missed me and hit the tree to my left. Grabbing the tree trunk with my hands, I swung my body around the tree to the right and struck him hard with my cleated right boot in the chest. To my utter surprise, he fell to the ground and did not move.

Glancing back to assure myself his companion was not coming, I carefully examined him, taking the sword first. The sword seemed to be made of ceramic material. After stripping him of weapons and equipment, I checked his breathing. I used my steel hunting knife I found on me earlier to check for hot breath after I saw how it worked for me. He was not breathing. Not knowing if he had a heart or pulse, I had to figure he was dead just from the breath check.

After watching again to see if his mate was coming, I took off my soiled Earth clothes and put on the outer parts of his uniform. It had good width for me, and the pants were easily rolled up for the length I needed. I decided to wear his helmet and sword in case the other soldier showed up. And I kept my knife where I could get it out quickly.

In respect for his near humanity, I decided not to leave his almost naked body just lying there. I picked up his body and carried it to a nearby low spot out of sight of the general path in which he had walked. There I used a shovel he had on him to cover his body evenly but moderately with dirt.

Fearing my discovery again, I put the shovel and my old clothes in his pack and headed carefully back to my shelter. I reasoned that the other soldier would circle the large hill to meet his friend halfway, so I wanted to quickly get to the side he started on, which was where my shelter was.

Moving along close to the base of the hill to be less noticeable, I prepared to round a huge boulder when I found the other soldier had just rounded the hill 15 feet in front of me. He was retracing his steps after his mate did not show up on the other side and was momentarily surprised to see this was not his friend, although I was wearing the uniform.

With a scream, he pulled his sword, and I pulled the one I took from the dead soldier. Both of us were at fever pitch to fight, and he stepped forward and swung to cut off my head. I ducked, catching his glancing blow off the helmet, then swung from left to right waist-high at him. He stepped aside and swung his sword to catch mine. My strength was greater than his, though he was a little taller, so my swing knocked his sword back. He turned all the way around and swung this time at my legs. I jumped over the sword and swung back at his head. He pulled his head back out of the way. He swung again from my left side and I blocked the blow with mine and rotated it over my head in an arch to the right side. Slightly off balance, he swung again across my chest, but I ducked under the swooping blade. Pulling my sword from my lower right, I aimed a swath across his ribs and chest. The blade caught him there, ripping his uniform but not drawing any blood. He was only phased for a moment. I quickly pulled out my knife and hurled it at his chest. He ducked, but it caught him in the shoulder. He looked frozen in shock for a moment, then collapsed to the ground.

This time my adrenaline was pumping mightily. I also collapsed to the ground, my mind racing to take this all in. I kept the sword ready just in case. Relying on techniques I must have learned in the past, I slowed down my breathing and did not feel sick to my stomach. Then I moved stealthily over to the soldier and checked him out like I did the first one. Removing my knife and his weapons from him, I then checked for breath. He too was dead.

Examining the short and very shallow cut on his chest and the shoulder wound, I did not see why the knife killed him. He was bleeding, but it was too incidental to be fatal. Two soldiers were dead from minor blows. *What is this?*

As I prepared to bury his body, I noticed he did not have the noticeable genital hump of males. When I examined him there, I found that he had no genitals at all! "He" was neither male nor female. Just a hole for urination. *Wow! This is really weird!*

I went ahead and placed the body next to the base of the hill there, shoveling dirt down from above. I also kept his equipment and picked it up to carry with the first set. Hurrying to my tiny home, I placed a supply of fruit and berries in one of the soldiers' packs, then as best I could I covered up the evidences of my presence there. I abandoned the cave quickly with all my baggage.

After a few hours of going through the brush farther away from the city, I came to a large lake with amazingly clear water. To the right was a set of hills, so I headed there, eating the fruit of bushes and trees along the way. After another hour, I reached the hills and found a small outcropping of rock within a mile of the lake, but out of direct sight. I felt very tired, so I threw the stuff in and began to examine the equipment I found on the soldiers. It was midafternoon, so I decided to search for more food after that, then I would prepare the shelter better.

Each soldier had the same equipment. I examined the equipment on the first one. He had a long and narrow two-edged sword of fine ceramic material resembling metal. His belt sported a ceramic knife. I also saw that he had a different kind of horn than the soldiers I saw yesterday, looking like it blew out lower pitched notes. Oddly, I did not find anything metallic in what they had. I suspected he and the other one from their looks were seasoned veterans who had not been out in the woods for some time and had prepared to be out for a few days. They had a small supply of packaged foods.

The weapons of each included a crossbow, about two dozen arrows, and a backpack full of shovels and similar tools for survival for a few days. *Maybe they were not looking for me after all.* Anyway, now I had their tools and would survive instead of them.

This last thought brought a painful flash of remembrance, a feeling of Deja Vu. My memories were blocked in most areas. I could only remember a few skills which helped me survive. They felt like instincts which were inborn and not learned, yet I knew they must have been part of my training or upbringing. For now, I could only trust these instinctive actions until my memories unfroze, if ever. I felt like a lost animal in a strange place. Past habits and practices were all I knew. If they were not appropriate in a future situation, then I may die or be seriously injured. I had nothing else.

Deep feelings of despair and self-pity pushed to wash over me. I could not connect them with anything. They were just there. I let them come and remain for a few minutes to see if they showed me anything. Nothing revealed itself, so I suppressed them for the moment and sought nearby food to go with the soldier's rations. They carried some new fruits and berries, along with what looked like baked bread. I ate the food I already trusted and added one bite of new fruit to see if I could tolerate it. I would do this with each new potential food until I knew what suited my Earth body.

"Earth." Somehow the word struck fear and loneliness into me. *Why? What am I doing here, and like this? Who am I?* Suddenly questions flooded into my mind like a dam breaking. I grabbed my head and fell to my knees from the pressure. *Who am I? Where am I? Who am I? Where am I? Who am I? Where am I? Who am I? Where am I?* Over and over. Tears came. Big tears. Heartbreak tears. I was afraid and lonely. Deep feelings. So deep. So strong. So heavy. I cried from deep despair. *Why? Why?* I did not know. I just sobbed, feeling deep pain and grief in my soul.

Finally, my deep sobbing began to ebb. I realized that something had happened to me, and I could not remember what it was. As darkness approached, bits and pieces of my education came to help me. *I have amnesia, probably from traumatic stress.* Some psychological trauma had struck me, and my only way to cope was to blank out all memories before the moment of the trauma. Training and education remained at my command, but I did not know where or how I learned what I knew. I just had to trust these unconscious instincts.

I surmised that the trauma must have been incredibly heavy. I decided to go easy on myself and not try to recover immediately. Such trauma must come back to consciousness slowly, or I could go into deeper amnesia and lose all touch with reality. *At least, that is what the education in my head says.* It sounded right, so I rested with what I knew so far and prepared the shelter site with the shovel for basing there and especially for sleep.

It felt good to weep openly as if trying to wash away grief, even though I knew that was not something that I normally did. It was a small step to recovery. *Yet who am I? Everyone has a name, so what is mine?* It would not come. This seemed so ominous and deep, but I had to set my thoughts and emotions aside for now. Stressing about it would not help me.

The last glimpses of twilight shown on the horizon. Those heavy thoughts after the rest of the day's happenings had used a lot of emotional energy. The heaviness of sleep came hard. I willingly surrendered to the deep rest of those who had worked a grueling day.

Chapter 3: Day Three – Coming to Terms

As I awakened the next day, I felt exhausted. The psychological load I was carrying was still there, and it was heavy. *Is it time to face the buried thoughts and memories?* Up until then, my only thoughts had been on survival. Anything else was too distracting.

I ate some of the soldiers' bread rations while I mulled over how to go about recapturing my memories. I thought about the dead soldiers whose death had enabled me to live better in the wild. Also, it felt weird that I was not more upset about killing them, even in self-defense. It really made me wonder what my previous life was like. And I remembered that I never enjoyed hunting on Earth unless someone ate the meat as food. Now I ate the food of those whom I had killed. These thoughts struck deep into my heart. My conscience was screaming. I suddenly stopped in mid-bite and spit it all out. I could not eat any more of their rations. The remainder of my light breakfast was furnished by the nearby trees and bushes.

I gathered up their rations and took them out to a spot with loose dirt. While burying them, my mind was free to consider how to work through my bizarre situation. By the time the last shovel of dirt was tamped onto the pile, I had worked up a process for studying the situation. After getting back to the shelter and sitting comfortably, I relaxed to process my thoughts.

First, I walked around myself mentally and looked from the outside. I tried thinking about different subjects from school and life. My mind contained knowledge of martial arts and military procedures, so I must have been trained in those areas. I was aware of nutrition and medical concepts in moderate measure, so I was at least into personal health. I had facility with mathematics and physical sciences, so I may have been a scientist or engineer. My personal awareness of myself psychological-ly on feelings, dreams and anxieties, and other persons, showed either considerable opportunity for self-analysis and growth or for training as a counselor or psychologist or both.

These areas were more than a typical soldier would have received in his education. I felt they show a rounded education which was beyond normal. The wide range of educational knowledge said I had a special purpose for which I trained for several years. Or perhaps my former training caused me to be chosen for a special mission?

Second, I looked at myself physically. I looked like a man in his late thirties to early forties, about six feet tall and around 200 pounds, slightly balding in front and back, and in good health as far as cardiovascular system and muscle tone. The world I was on had slightly weaker gravity than Earth, and so I felt quite strong and agile. I felt I could easily run two miles in under nine minutes. My hands were strong yet flexible with soft skin, so hard labor with my hands was not in my past. Fingertip calluses indicated much typing, and a callus on the inside of the last knuckle of the tall finger verified much handwriting. Also, martial art calluses were slight, so I wondered if such training came late. Only to face what this world offered? Or could it had been to face problems on Earth before this world? So many possibilities!

At the thought of Earth, I felt strangely anxious. I shuddered and saw gooseflesh on my arms. During this self-analysis, the thought of Earth and two other subjects caused me to feel extremely uneasy. The first of the others was when I began to touch on personal beliefs and philoso-phy. The last was at the end when I decided I was there on a mission. To think of religion and the meaning and purpose of human life caused me to breathe heavy and want to run. The idea that I might had been sent there made me want to scream out in anguish of soul.

Starting to lose emotional control again, I backed off mentally and did some exercises and relaxation techniques. I had a vague desire to pray, but for some reason I was resisting doing it. I took a jog to calm my emo-tions, gathering some more fruits and berries in a bag for later. I decided that after I completed the analyzing process that I would approach the fearful subjects again. And I would do it slowly, very slowly.

As I ran, careful to look all around, I looked at the third part, this world. It looked like a large planet circling twin yellow suns. I also felt the twin suns were always over the equator, and so there were no changing seasons. My location appeared to be near the equator. I could not tell about the annual path around the twin suns compared to the 12 Earth months. The twin suns were visible in much the same way as on Earth, and each day was about 23 hours long.

The atmosphere was thinner than Earth, but must have contained a higher percentage of oxygen, because I breathed freely and naturally. The delicacy of the towering trees showed there was little or no wind, and there must be no snow or ice during the year. The temperature was about 65 degrees F. at night and no more than 75 degrees F. at midday. Direct sunlight felt mild, and I had not burned or tanned, so ultraviolet light levels must have been low.

How long have I been here? Days? Weeks? Something told me I had only known this world a short while. The main evidence was that my sleep cycle had not fully adjusted to the 23-hour days. So far, I had seen no animals or insects which bother humans as on Earth. All the animals had been eating plants, even one large sloth like creature. Their teeth were obviously for plants only. Bat like birds with wide wings ate berries and leaves in the treetops and in the bushes.

I saw a dead animal which started growing moss overnight where it lay. Fast growing plant life was apparently how decaying flesh was handled. There was a little smell of bacterial action as well.

The thought of strange bacteria bothered me. The defeat of the aliens through Earth's bacteria in <u>The War of the Worlds</u> by H. G. Wells came to mind. I decided to contemplate disease later, ... if ever. I could only hope that strange bacteria would not be harmful to me there, and also that my own bacteria would not be a problem to that world's biological life.

Back at my shelter and cooling off slowly because of the thin atmosphere, I began to look at the final area of questions. *How far back does my memory go?* That was potentially frightening, so I proceeded cautiously. I could remember only to several minutes before I burst through the door to the wall of the city. I remembered my head pounding and feeling dizzy. I had started out in tears and screaming, holding my face in my hands. Two aliens were standing fully erect with shocked looks on their faces. We were in what looked like a makeshift control room, and no one was touching me. I was standing beside them in front of a 17-inch television monitor. Something I had just seen or experienced must have caused me severe emotional pain, since I remembered no physical pain and had no wounds at all.

Suddenly, I had distrusted the aliens and ran out of the room, then blocked the door to keep them inside. I ran quickly to a furnished room with artistic furniture, apparently my room as a guest there. I had thrown on a huge backpack and sizable front pack, then tossed some other items into two large bags with straps which I threw over each shoulder. Looking each way, I left the room determined to fight for my life to escape. I searched around for a while, avoiding aliens until I found the outside wall of the city. When no aliens were visible, I went to the door and tried to open it. It was frozen shut from little use. A few hard shoves and it was open. My survival experience away from the aliens began then.

The amnesia appeared to have occurred in that control room. It was still too painful to think about it then. Besides, something else caught my attention. Since leaving the city, I had carried those four items with me and not given them much thought until this moment. I carried them with me to both shelters, but all they had done was take up space.

I turned and looked at the baggage in the corner of my tiny home. *Why have I not investigated these or used them before now?* I was wearing and using the tools and clothes of the soldiers who fought me. Yet everything I needed must surely be in those packs and bags. And there I was sitting at the other end of the shelter gazing at them as if they had disappeared and just re-appeared out of thin air. Then I felt anger welling up inside me. *How much more craziness must I deal with in myself?*

I fumed for a while, then I realized that the anger was doing nothing for me, and so I took some slow deep breaths to regain composure. Then I looked again at the four bags and packs. I went over and put my arms around them. They felt precious to my arms and chest then.

Feeling deep grief, I let myself go into sobbing like a lost child. *What is happening? Where am I? What do I do now?* After sobbing for some time, I felt better. I knew from my psychological background this was good for me. I wished I knew where all that was leading me.

I took a short walk to limber up while eating some of the abundant food.

"These fruits and berries are everywhere,"

I said aloud. It sounded strange to hear my voice. After the walk, I settled down to open the bags I brought with me.

Two of the parcels were like duffel bags, and two were back packs, one medium sized for the front and one oversized pack for the rear. Each was made of tough denim, the normal duffel bag material on Earth. The two smallest appeared to be made in this world from tough but different cloth.

After staring at them for a while, I opened the front backpack first. Reaching in to pull each item out without seeing the rest of the items in the bag, the first handful I pulled out was clothing. It was lightweight and compact, what I must have brought from Earth with me. Closer examination revealed more clothing like this, amounting to several changes of outfits, with no chilly weather gear. Some were camouflaged and some were dressy, but most were casual.

A typical casual outfit was a one-piece suit with short sleeves and long pants. The base color was khaki. Green rings one inch wide wrapped around each sleeve and pant cuff. A green stripe of elastic three inches wide went around the waist. The collar was cut as a V-neck with a one-inch wide green border. The outfit used silent Velcro instead of zippers or buttons.

A small pouch had some vanity supplies, such as shavers and tooth cleaning equipment. It seemed like I had been there less than one month so far. Thus, it was clear I was here for some mission or trip with a purpose, but not for a long time. I thought the other items in the pouches would tell me more.

I put that backpack aside after repacking it and decided to let the others wait until tomorrow. The emotions were already too strong. Also, it was getting darker, so night was coming again. I could not bear to look inside the rest of the bags just then, but I believed focusing on them was a good sign that the process of recovery had begun. I pulled them around me like beloved pets. Holding them close and wondering what answers and nightmares they contained, I lay awake for a while before falling asleep.

Chapter 4: Day Four - Discovery

I awakened with my last dream of the night still vividly in mind. In the dream, I awoke screaming on a table in a surgical room. As I sat up yelling, I saw my dearest friend and slowly stopped screaming as he held my arm and talked calmly to me. He and I were the only ones in the room, but I felt we were being watched through one-way mirrors. I got off the surgical table feeling painfully sore all over, wearing a hospital gown open in the back. He helped me down as I pulled the gown around my body. We walked over to look out the window to the left. It was sundown, but we could see violence and turmoil in the street below. Inside the window in front of us was a globe of the Earth, sitting on a Bible. I picked up the globe, and the Bible opened by itself on the table to the Revelation to John. The globe collapsed in my hands, with blood flowing out of it onto my wrists and forearms. Soon it was a gooey mess on my arms, slopping onto the floor. I looked to my friend for help, and he was gone. As I looked back to the globe, my hands were clean, because it and the room had disappeared. I was floating in dark space alone with no stars. At that point, I awoke in fear soaked in perspiration and ready to run or fight.

I breathed deeply and rubbed my hands through my hair, wondering what this meant about my past. *Has something happened to the Earth, or to my friend? Has some part of Bible prophecy come into play? Am I truly alone here?* The dream provided vague hints of answers to some of the questions I was afraid to face consciously. I was starting to remember bits and pieces. Would the full revelation overcome me when it came? I shuddered.

Gaining composure, I looked again at the four bags and packs I was still clutching. I set them aside and went to get some fresh food and water. I took a short walk to limber up while eating and then settled down to open the other three bags.

Back in my shelter, I put aside the front backpack that I examined last night and opened the smaller duffel bag, ready for personal items to pop out. I knew I could stop at any time if the pain and fear become too much.

The first item I pulled out was a picture encased in plastic. It showed a smiling woman, a teenage girl, a teenage boy, and a happy man. I recognized the man as myself, and the woman and children were my family.

They looked so good to me! Oh, how I wanted to hold them! Memories came flooding back of periods spent grilling out and picnics at parks and vacations at the ocean and mountains. Times then were cozy and casual, living in a house which contained many computerized luxuries and robot machines for labor around the house. Other memories came of later times living in fear. Flashes of moments included traveling in ground vehicles at night with a few possessions, scenes in a mountain village, and times in caves holding each other closely and singing hymns and silly songs to laugh.

A few other people had been around, and I remembered them with longing as being precious to me. One slightly older man had been a dear friend, the one in my dream. I saw scenes of us talking excitedly about some ideas or projects. When I saw a scene of us gazing at a monitor in a laboratory, the memories ceased. I found I was looking at the far hill in this world in front of my shelter, back from my daydream.

As I reached into the pack again, I pulled out a soft book of some type. It was an old study Bible, New International Version. Inside was this note,

To my grandson, Daniel, from your Grandpa Mike. I am so proud of you finishing your high school degree program so quickly. May this wonderful book inspire you as it has me. Keep it safe and hide its words in your heart. June 12, 2024

Many verses were underlined and highlighted. The underlining appeared to be Grandpa's, and the highlighting appeared to be mine. Most of the highlights were in the New Testament, and the Revelation to John was heavily highlighted.

The Bible felt like a dear friend. In my mind an impulse came to turn to a certain verse in the Gospel of John. The verse that came to me was

John 13:7, but I did not remember ever memorizing it. Flipping to it, I read where Christ said,

What I do you do not realize now, but you shall understand hereafter.

These words provided strange peace and comfort. My heart felt like warm oil was flowing over it. Instantly, I felt less alone.

I laid the Bible aside and reached inside the duffel bag again. This time I pulled out what looked like a pocket computer. I recognized it as the first part of my electronic wallet, or ewallet. I put it on my neck as a loose neckband, and then put the second part on my left wrist. Here were the details I had wanted yet dreaded. Taking a deep breath, I placed my right thumb on the sensor pad on my wrist and looked into its retina scanner. The screen asked if I wanted voice input, brain wave scanning, or keyboard. I answered aloud, "Voice." The device then asked by screen if I wanted answers back by screen, voice, or high-speed earphone. Again, I told it to speak aloud.

It answered from the neckband in a copy of my voice, "Hello, Dr. Davidson. How may I help You?"

SO THAT'S MY NAME!

I was temporarily taken aback when the device said, "Hello, Dr. Davidson. How may I help You?" With that one jolt many memories came flooding in, just as if a computer were booted up and lights began flickering on. Yet they came back in a jumble and only partially. I took a deep breath and decided to probe with some simple questions.

"What is my full name?"

"Daniel Wayne Davidson."

"What is my home country?"

"The United States of America."

"What is my hometown?"

"Tampa, Florida."

"Where do I now live?"

"Present location is in the mountains of central North Dakota. Two years before that you were in western Montana."

"I believe I am on a planet orbiting twin stars. Where am I exactly?"

"This is password protected. Password, please."

Well! An important piece of data, and my amnesia held me back from conquering my amnesia! I paused to take a few deep breaths to see if a word or phrase came to me. "Maranatha, Apocalypse now," came to mind, so I spoke it.

"Password accepted. You are on the planet Ontario circling the twin suns Andromeda SF16 217A and B."

"How did this planet get its name?"

"Your Canadian friend, Maurice Yves Monterre, named it when you and he first discovered it."

Maurice! More memories. And tears. Why I did not know. Having started this series of questions, I could not stop now.

"Why am I here on Ontario?"

"You are here to form a friendship with the Ontarian Kamikini in hopes of bringing your family and friends here to live in relative peace."

After that I turned it off to think for a while. It said it had 98% power left, and I was glad to see that. I tightened my silent Velcro shoelaces and jogged around the hill to clear my head and let these revelations sink in. Something must be happening on Earth to make me want to leave it for another world. Also, how did I get there, and how could I bring my family? I needed to know a lot more. But first, I ate lunch and opened the rest of my gear.

After the light meal, I emptied the rest of the first duffel bag. The remaining contents were also personal effects, except for a canister of computer discs. These contained a wealth of knowledge for my use and for the Kamikini. I counted 15 discs, enough to contain a vast amount of data. If the Kamikini are behind technologically compared to Earth, this much information would push them decades, even centuries, ahead.

I put the items back into the duffel bag and shoved it next to the front backpack. Then I opened the oversized backpack. It contained a variety of survival gear of the latest miniaturized sophistication, including a robotic machine for medical diagnostics and surgical repairs. The collection featured dehydrated foods in vacuum pouches, a modified geodesic dome tent, other robotic repair machines, a laser cutting torch, a second electronic wallet, a lightweight plastic suit of armor that came as an automatically deploying unit, and a variety of weapons and ammunition, and tools to make more ammunition. There were laser weapons, dart guns, land mines, grenades, a semi-automatic scope rifle with silencer, and a silencer pistol with a full magazine. All compact and lightweight, except for some of the ammunition.

Putting everything back into it, I shoved it aside and reached for the last bag, the bigger duffel bag. It contained even more weapons. Between the two packs, there was enough to outfit a small squad of at least 10 soldiers with lightweight weapons. There was enough to defeat a platoon and also destroy a building. Or for one man to do so, much like the late Twentieth Century movie heroes. Really? Am I here on a mission to kill other creatures on a massive scale? Is my goal to destroy some alien beings to steal their homes and bring my friends here in their place? The negative questions were so terrible that I had to know the rest of what the ewallet would tell me.

"Wallet, why did I bring all these weapons?"

"You intend to help the Kamikini defeat their enemies, the Makurani. Then Ontario should be in permanent peace, and the Kamikini will hopefully allow you to bring your friends and family here to live."

"Why do I want to leave Earth?"

"To escape the worldwide religious persecution and violence against Christians."

"Wallet, how recent is your memory?"

"The last time you programmed me was on Earth the day before you jumped to Ontario by gravitational angle shifting. The date was 2055 July 3."

After that, I switched to input by brain waves and high-speed earphone to learn as much as I could quickly. I found out how I was able to jump through space, where the jump vehicle was hidden, the location of two caches of weapons I had previously stocked, how my friends and I had scouted out this world, and about the details we understood of this world. My wrist screen also had a rough GPS map of this part of the planet that we had made using drones. The screen unfolded to twice its width and height when requested. I realized my whole reason for coming had been to meet the Kamikini, befriend them, and then defend them. So why did I run away?

Too many questions without answers. My thoughts were running in several directions at once. It was past sundown. The answers had to wait a little longer while I gave all these pieces of data a chance to sink in.

I set up two motion detectors that would send vibratory signals to my neckband. Then I settled in for some more restless sleep.

Chapter 5: Day Five - Warfare

The next day brought with it a new sense of hope. Having some of the fragments of my memory come together helped me get up with less stiffness and a little pleasure at being alive. I was more in tune with the surrounding beauty. Birds whistled their strange calls, and small animals chirped and scurried about. And yet there was also an underlying anger about the state of the Earth, along with my frustration at having amnesia forced upon me somehow.

Sitting outside the shelter in the early light, I enjoyed the fruits and berries picked the day before for breakfast, along with the cool water from the creek. Like an athlete at a great meet, I found my senses were heightened for the adventure of the day. I expected to further unravel what had happened, shuddering with excitement as I settled down to look again at this mystery. Since I had some idea why I came, I first wondered why I ran away from the Kamikini like I did. *Did I discover something hideous about them? Did they show me something grotesque?* I was not sure I could trust them. Without my memory, I felt better for then only trusting my wits and instincts more than trusting other creatures, especially if my home planet was hostile. Also, it appeared I was not trusting of the Makurani even before I came. *So, where does a man alone go to find himself and learn the truth about his situation in a strange world?*

Something made me check in the packs again. I had seen some kind of electronic box, so I dug it out and took a good look at it. I soon remembered that it was a radio controller for drones. Also, it was still communicating with drones that had been sent out. I must have flown them to the cities and landed them in places where they would not be found. As I played with the box for a while, I found that there were 12 drones that I had placed in the cities, and they were recording anything that sounded like speech. The drone controller box was connected to another box wirelessly, and it was a speech translator device. *Maybe I have already been learning their language.*

On the other side, I wondered if the Kamikini would be friendly if I changed back to my own clothes and approached them carefully. I did not know why I ran away, though. How would I let them know I wanted to communicate with them?

As I walked around thinking about this outside the shelter, I heard sounds off to my left just around the side of the hill. Swiftly, yet carefully, I ran back inside the shelter. I grabbed the semi-automatic scope rifle with silencer, a couple of fragmentation grenades, and one of their swords in its sheath. I crouched behind some bushes and edged closer to the sound.

Looking through the branches, I scanned the area and saw 12 Makurani soldiers in their red and gold uniforms. They looked like they were on a search mission. Each was trying to be silent, moving slowly through the forest and open field. Despite that, several days in the open had made it easy for me to pick out strange sounds, however faint. The closest ones, as seen through the scope, looked profoundly serious. They did not seem to be on a practice march. They scanned the area around carefully, moving forward as different ones motioned them by hand signals. One up front was looking intently to scout the area. I hid well whenever he looked my way.

I decided to test their intentions and give myself some advantages in case I was the object of the hunt. Backtracking to the shelter, I took a piece of my Earth clothing, a casual suit, and wet it from my water pouch. I placed it on a bush ahead of the soldiers to look as if it was put there to dry out. Then I circled around their right flank and watched from about 100 feet away. I found a spot slightly behind where they should find the suit.

Soon one of them spotted the suit and motioned to the others. While the others waited where they were, the group that saw it went to it carefully, then got down low and became noticeably quiet. Each loaded his crossbow, then they proceeded carefully in the direction of the tracks I made. They crouched and moved slowly in four sets of three.

They are definitely hunting for me. What if they did not intend harm but were just afraid? However, since two already had attacked me, I felt they would do the same. I did not have the luxury of taking my life in my hands and approaching 12 soldiers ready to fire, hoping they would not. My being there may have been to help my family and friends, so I knew I had to take an approach which assured my safety. It pained me to think about it, but I knew I had to surprise and eliminate this squad of armed enemies. They were too close to my supplies for me to simply pack up my things and get away from them. I also could not just run off and let these hostile beings find and take my arsenal which was obviously brought from Earth for me to use.

They were all moving past me in an open field of low bushes in a line about 75 feet away. Each group of three was about 25 feet apart. As the third group passed my location, I decided to take out the last trio of soldiers quickly. Using the semi-automatic silencer rifle, I sighted them in and wondered if their anatomy was like humans. To be sure I had a kill shot, I triggered a round into the rear soldier in the neck. When he went limp and fell immediately without uttering a sound, I then hit his partners in the neck when they turned to look at him. They fell immediately in the same way. The next group of three in front of them easily collapsed with three more shots.

So far it was quick and easy, just like stacking blocks. Without pausing, I took out the set next to the front. By this time, the three in the lead had discovered their fellows had crumpled awkwardly. The two who stood up straighter to look back soon received rounds in the chest which threw them backwards. The remaining soldier stayed down and was out of my sight.

Anxiety jumped on me like a tiger. The last one could be the most dangerous. He was probably the leader and was the most experienced. His skills might enable him to compensate for my superior weapons if I relaxed. *I need to find him now! Where is he?* I strained to look through the scope all around his spot to locate him.

As I caught him in my scope, I saw him aiming his crossbow in my direction. He had judged the direction of the shots and was watching for something at which to shoot. I was exposed enough for him to see me, and I saw in the scope an arrow that was coming. I jerked to the right swiftly. His shot nicked my skin at the left ribs, passing under my left arm. I got up quickly to catch him in my sights again. He was scrambling to my right, running farther away. He was grabbing for his horn to warn others. Two quick shots found their mark. His body lay still.

Since he had wanted to use his horn, I felt others were within ear shot, and so I looked quickly around to see if they were in sight. Also scanning the field with the scope showed no one else around. Relieved, my mind shouted thoughts and feelings at me. Killing them did not feel good, even though I was fairly mechanical while doing it. I did not like destroying other intelligent beings. *Do they also know the Creator?* I lowered the rifle and leaned against a rock for a moment to ponder this sadly.

The sting of the arrow cut brought me out of my thoughts and back to where I stood with rifle in hand. I put a quick bandage on it as I listened carefully for any other sounds. After a few minutes, I looked at each soldier in my scope and saw each where he had fallen. Starting with the leader, I then worked my way carefully over to each and examined him. I noticed each face and checked each wound.

After examining the first three trios, I crouched down to look at the last set. As I bent down, I heard something make a whizzing sound as it flew over my head toward the right. I looked quickly to see an arrow passing on into the bushes.

I jumped to the right of a thick bush and peered through it toward the direction from which the arrow came. A barrage of arrows was passing overhead and behind me. I vaguely saw figures loading crossbows and then running toward me.

They were closely bunched but some were closer to me than others. Instinctively, I pulled out a shrapnel grenade and armed it. When the closest one was about 30 feet away, I threw it from behind the bush past him about 20 feet. It was a fragmentation type with steel pellets around it, so I went flat on the ground.

For a small grenade, it gave a fierce explosion which hurt my ears and made me feel it thump the ground. When the flying dirt and branches had settled a bit after so many pellets went flying, I got back up and looked over the bush. No one was advancing. Pointing the rifle straight ahead, I slowly rose. I saw no movement. I halted my breathing and heard nothing but my ears ringing a little.

My feet were unsteady, and my heart was pounding, but I strode to the first soldier. He was clearly dead. Each soldier I checked was dead. There were 13 killed by the blast. I wondered if the two separate groups had made up one full platoon of 25.

A new puzzle lay before me. Although a few of the soldiers were mangled, the wounds on the other soldiers would not be more than flesh wounds on humans. All had at least one pellet from the grenade that penetrated their skin. But why did all of them die? Then I remembered the loudness of the explosion, and it made me feel I was still in danger. These ponderings about their wounds would have to wait.

Concerned that another group would show up at some point, I swiftly got more grenades and ammo out of the shelter and went back. I dragged each body to a low place nearby and used a small dirt throwing power tool to cover them up. I gathered up their weapons and recovered the suit decoy. Then I paused to wonder whether their superiors would know their trip plans and send a team to investigate their failure to return.

As I jogged back to the shelter, I decided to change into my Earth clothes and keep the ones I was wearing in case I needed them later. Back at the shelter, I healed my slight wound with the healing robot, then I changed. My own clothes were better camouflage than the red and gold uniform, anyway.

I found the ewallet was recording aspects of what was happening to me as I went along, and so I recorded a log of the events as I had experienced them. After that, an idea came to me that soon caused a plan to form in my head. Rather than hide and wait to be surprised, I would take the initiative and find both the Kamiki city and the Makura city which were closest to me. Then I would redistribute my weapons to several locations between the two cities. In case a group of soldiers discovered me, I would always have a supply of extra weapons nearby. And if a hidden cache was found, I would set up a boobytrap to destroy it and the ones who discovered it. However, I already noted that the guns and rifles used my handgrip and fingerprints to unlock them. Also, the GPS unit showed I had a stash several miles away, so I decided to check it out before long.

After packing a selection of weapons, I retraced the path to the Kamiki city and found it about 10 miles west of my shelter. (West was what I called that direction by assuming the twin suns which were slightly off vertical were to the south at their highest point.) Along the way I saw two companies of Makura soldiers which I avoided. It took much time walking in the overgrown grass and underbrush beside the main roads.

By the time I returned to my shelter, it was dark. After setting the field security system, I was able to relax. Sleep came quickly.

Chapter 6: Day Six and Beyond – Learn and Prepare

The next day I used the GPS to locate the city of the Makurani soldiers, and it was about 15 miles northeast of my shelter. I scouted it out and fell back about 3 miles toward my main shelter and hid a supply of gear and weapons. Then I went three more miles and placed some more.

After setting up a tent and spending the night there, I took down the tent and headed back to my main shelter. I grabbed most of the remaining weapons and placed half about three miles from the Kamikini city and the rest about three more miles out. This provided a stock of supplies in four locations. If pursued from either city, I could retreat toward the other and defend myself at several points. I also knew I had the two other caches somewhere that could be used as needed, but I did not know yet just how much was in each of them.

When I placed the two closest caches near each city, I took a brief look at the city from outside and noticed they were surprisingly similar. About 10,000 people was the capacity of each. The walls were three-quarter mile long on each side with a square footprint. They were of tan clay construction and had walls 60 feet high. There were three gates or doors in each wall. Each city's main gate was facing East and had a paved road of soft material for walking traffic which extended out directly toward the other city. This eastern wall had an open field reaching out into farmland flanked by forest. The other walls had a 100-yard clear space which ended at the forest's edge.

Soldiers from both cities continued to scan the countryside all along my way. Watching and avoiding soldiers made my journey long and slow. I did not want to meet any others if I could help it.

As I was traveling, I listened to the Makura drone recordings to pick out any vocabulary and sentence structure I could. I also learned how to interpret most of the horn signals. It struck me how the language resembled Hawaiian in sound and structure. I was also surprised at how quickly I was learning it. *I must have worked on this before.* When I could, I watched videos of conversations to improve my pronunciation.

For the next few days back at the main shelter, I did nothing but watch videos and listen to conversations to memorize vocabulary. The ewallet had a language helper, so I loaded it up as I learned words. Inside a week I had learned many basic words, including the rule to add "ni" to most words to make the plural.

I found out the hostile city was named Hekanalo. Some conversations mentioned the alien being which had killed 27 soldiers with strange weapons and must be in league with the Kamikini. They thought the alien was hiding out near the Kamiki city. The directives were to find him and kill him in whatever way they could. Shortly after this command was given, I overheard details of their plans. That gave me a tremendous advantage over them, and I had even more incentive to master their language.

I found out they assumed I would not be nearby at this time, so I was able to stay nearby and watch their movements easily. Observing them near the city, I saw them practicing their war maneuvers. They were so very skillful they reminded me of the oriental martial artists of Earth. Each one appeared to be a seasoned veteran. By getting close at times, I also learned some of the basic counting numbers.

After a few days, I had also learned the Kamiki city I ran from was Kohilo. It appeared for the moment that all of either group's people lived in just these two cities. *Someday I may try to find out if other groups live on Ontario.*

When I heard their plans on when to send out a larger force of soldiers, I decided to move closer to the Kamikini city two days ahead of them. They were planning to send out about 500 in groups of 25, mostly searching about Kohilo in patterns described in their spoken directives.

As I prepared to go back toward Kohilo, I moved my main shelter three miles farther south to make it more unlikely the Makurani would find it. At the new site, I heard the horns of the Makurani, especially as their soldiers got closer. Their city horn sounds got fainter as I moved away from Hekanalo. Setting up a schedule to watch the drone videos of the Makurani, I began to think more about the Kamikini.

How would I learn the Kamikini language? I checked the ewallet and found it already contained some basic vocabulary for their language. Playing with it for a while showed their language was the same as that of the Makurani. This was extremely fortunate and would help me communicate easily with either group. I merged the ewallet language info into one set of vocabulary.

As I pondered this fortunate development, I traveled and hid myself that afternoon near the main gates of Kohilo. Soldiers from Makurani were all about in the woods, so I had to be cautious at every moment. I saw two soldiers from Kohilo in their blue and silver uniforms leave the city. They headed into the woods, so I followed them. They ignored the Makurani and went to a lake not far away and took off their clothes for a swim. I listened to their relaxed banter and found I could make out several of the words and phrases.

I then used a roundabout path to my new main shelter to hide my trail in case they or someone else tried to follow me. I tried to make it look like no one else had been near the lake but was not sure how well they could figure it out.

Soon I was listening to the Kamikini recordings. In just a few sentences, I found their language was indeed the same as the Makurani. I wondered if the Kamikini could pick up any horn sounds from Hekanalo, and vice versa.

A noticeable difference between the two cities was that Kamikini conversations were more positive and upbeat, yet at times they seemed to sing songs about a time of great grief that they had all suffered. The Makurani conversations were stern and dealt with harsh themes. It reminded me of the ancient cities of Sparta and Athens in Greece. Similar people but opposite traits and lifestyles.

Remembering the last few days of language immersion, I mentally put together a picture of the two groups and their relationship. Some of the Makurani had talked about having questioned the Kamikini concerning the alien. The Kamikini must had said quite truthfully that I had come, and also showed my stuff to them. They said I had left suddenly when I saw something on a flat square which caused me to become terribly upset. Then they had described how I left the city, and that no one in Kohilo had seen me since. I was surprised and perplexed that they were so compliant and submissive.

It was then that the Makurani stepped up their search for me. They had found the two places where I killed their soldiers, as well as both of my earlier shelters near the battle sites. They kept mentioning the 27 killed to spur their troops to work harder to find me. Their values included duty, discipline, blind obedience to leadership, and arduous work. Fun and recreation were never mentioned.

The conversations in Kohilo were more peaceful and even playful. They valued the aesthetic and beautiful in nature and each other. They spoke of contentment and the enjoyment of simple pleasures. The only mention of the alien was to pray for his safety and soundness of mind. Again, there were moments when they seemed to all recount their shared time of great grief.

After a day of listening to Kamikini transmissions, I found my emotions jumping around all day. I listened for signs of deceitfulness or dishonesty. In the end, after hours of listening to get a "feel" for them, I decided it was time to reach out in trust to them. Although I had often found it necessary to be wary of people who seemed overly nice, I felt I must try to contact them soon.

When I prepared for bed in my shelter, I felt very alone, caught between two strange peoples. I still could not remember specifics of the traumatic situation that caused my amnesia. The Kamikini surely knew, but could I really trust them? My ewallet told me why I came here, but it could not tell me if something dreadful had previously happened on Earth, why I ran away from Kohilo, or why I was queasy about spiritual things.

I felt like a powerful animal on its own. Superior to my fellow creatures yet hungering for companionship. My desire to survive overpowered the need for others just then. My desire for communication with the Creator was held in check. I pondered these concerns for some time after dark, then drifted off to sleep.

The next morning, I awoke perspiring in great fear from a nightmare. I dreamed I was being carried by the Makurani and being forced to look at the screen which had caused me to lose my memory. At the moment I was placed kicking and screaming in front of the screen, I awoke and jumped out of my covers.

The horrible feelings of terrible loneliness, stark terror, and a strong angry rage were almost overpowering. The natives in the dream were evil beings who were intent on insuring I went mad.

This intensified my desire to be careful in any dealings with either set of the natives. After that dream, I despaired for a while about my whole situation. Then a flash of insight helped me develop a plan of action to ensure my first meeting with a native would be on my own terms and within my own circle of strength.

The next two days I spent preparing a meeting place of my choosing and then stocking the hidden storage places between the two cities with clothing and food from Earth. While at each site, I reexamined the weapons in the boxes and found a few unknown items. At site one going from Kohilo to Hekanalo I found a particularly delightful tool. What I had supposed to be a type of electrical battery was much more than that. It was a flying device with an atom cruncher energy generator. I was excited beyond words.

This opened up a lot of the memories still hidden. I remembered that the energy generator had been a recent marvel. A scientist had theoretically determined a practical way to convert all the mass of atoms into energy in 2047. It was the greatest breakthrough technologically since Germany had made the first practical fusion reactor in 2003. I heard an American laboratory had developed a working model in 2048, but it was as large as a supermarket. Then in early 2055, I opened a package and found a note from my friend Maurice saying,

SURPRISE! This is the prototype of the energy generator I have been working on secretly at the lab. I knew you might need every tool possible in your small set of packs. I took out some food to include this and a gravitational flying machine I developed in 2053. Employ them and enjoy them when you need to. I just hope you don't need the food first! Good luck, my dear friend.

Happy Flying!
Maurice

Ordinarily, the gravitational flying apparatus would take a heavy fission power supply for a person to use it in a flying machine. And yet there I was with a phenomenal power supply weighing in at 12 pounds!

The sheer joy of having such a tool given by my friend brought a tear to my eye. Nothing could had been more desirable to me. At this point in my stay on Ontario, no single other gift would have meant more. Maurice had known it, too.

I looked away and thought about what was happening to me. I was remembering many events from my past on Earth which came in fragments, although the whole was still muddled. I then remembered Maurice was my best friend, a man of like mind philosophically and scientifically. We were fellow engineers and research scientists who delighted in innovative technology in biomedicine and other fields while lamenting the horrid ways some of them were used by the federal government and the private sector. Only Maurice could know how much playing with these new toys would thrill me. What a friend!

The last few days I also heard on both cities' drone recordings references to a "Lohana". Lohana was a type of holiday, and this one was a high day or especially important one. All the soldiers from both cities were recalled to their homes for the two days of the Lohana. The Kamikini would spend their days in prayer and simple thankfulness, accompanied by laments over their losses. The Makurani would restock their field rations and hear motivational speeches about finding the alien. Both groups would stay inside their cities until the morning after Lohana.

Tomorrow was the holiday. No one would be looking for me. The meeting place was ready, but no one would be able to come for at least two days. At first, this was really frustrating after all my preparations. Then I thought about my feverish activity for the last week and decided I just might take a holiday too.

Chapter 7: Lohana and a New Encounter

When I awoke, I remembered it was Lohana. My plans were in place, and I had been working compulsively to prepare for any attack by Ontarian creatures. When the time was right, I would meet the Kamikini on my terms. The feverish, fairly paranoid, activity for so many days had left me nearly exhausted. I could take a breather now, then begin to approach the Kamikini. I believed a two-day vacation was in order.

I resolved to refresh my body and soul with travel and play. Tomorrow I would relax to also refresh my spirit deeply. Yesterday I found the gravitational sky lifter Maurice gave me and brought it back to my current shelter. I would play with it and scout out the country as well, but mostly for fun. I could be serious in a couple of days.

It was time to test the sky lifter to see how it worked and how I could fly with it. It assembled itself automatically from the foot pad, with the other parts unfolding from an arc around the feet, with a full-front shield to reduce air drag. I marveled at its compact size. It had a small foot plate large enough to spread the feet a little to distribute body mass. A telescoping pole came up to the back of the shoulders. A hollow bar shaped almost in a circle with one quadrant missing was hinged in the middle and attached to the pole near the middle of the back to swing up and forward to provide armrests and better mass distribution. The main control unit was located just above the hinge at mid-back. An earphone and mouthpiece in a helmet enabled voice commands. A headband inside the helmet allowed thought commands. Straps held the feet, legs, waist, and shoulders firmly. They detached automatically and quickly upon a series of voice commands. The gravity center was adjustable from knee level to neck. The energy generator was attached to the body instead of to the lifter. It could also be used to power the weapons such as lasers and electrical aids carried along.

I put on the lifter and generator. My first effort to flew flipped me over because I forgot to set the gravity center. I laughed at my awkward try. How my wife would giggle if she could see me! My second try went better, and with a little practice I learned how to adjust the center of gravity in midair. Soon I could fly a few yards off the ground at low speed.

Hearing the verbal information Maurice programmed into the ewallet, I soon was flying above the treetops at 50 mph. What a thrill! I played around for over three hours, trying out swirls, loops, wide circles, tight circles, midair stop-and-goes, and fast accelerations straight up. Daring to go up to two miles above the ground at one point revealed a spectacular view of the forested and hilly landscape. Then I headed out to a distant spot toward the South seen from high up. Careful to fly over only forested areas, I avoided inhabitants of the two cities.

From the Kamiki farmlands I had gathered some vegetable and fruits enough for two days of picnicking. I loaded a front pack with food and personal stuff. A backpack was loaded with weapons and supplies in case I met hostile creatures and also to try them out from midair. I could hardly wait to get away!

After lunch, I left in the lifter to fly south again. From Maurice's instructions, I should be able to accelerate straight up at the opposite of the gravitational pull of this world. Maximum upward or horizontal speed with air drag on Ontario would be over 250 mph, but the onboard processor adjusted acceleration to maintain a bearable speed under 100 mph. Speeds over that required explicit commands. I set the center of gravity at neck level to lean me forward for best view and proceed south, soon flying at 60 mph at 1,000 feet up.

I noticed as I went that there were other cities which appeared to be abandoned. They had walls in bad repair and were taken over by native vegetation. Many looked like they had not had inhabitants for many decades, or even centuries.

In about two hours I stopped at a foothill of a mountain range which had a lake like Big Bear Lake east of Los Angeles in California. The lake was 3,000 feet up and had trees taller than near the cities, some over 200 feet tall. In a beautiful spot which would let me see the setting of the twin suns, I settled down for a pleasant picnic by the lake. After the meal, I prepared a shelter up in a tree about 30 feet off the ground. The suns were setting and washing waves of light upon the peaceful lake.

With baroque music from Earth playing softly from my wallet into my earphones, I went peacefully into sleep.

The next morning, I awakened with a deep peace inside and a hunger to express thankfulness for my provisions to this point. After I prepared a campfire and ate a light breakfast, I took my Bible and sat by the campfire. I meditated on the many events which had occurred on Ontario until then. I had great hope I would fully recover my memories and finish the work I came here to do. I believed my family and friends would benefit from it. I just could not remember how for sure. Yet the hope was there inside.

I read for some time. Several passages spoke right to me. Walking beside the lake and reading aloud, I felt like the psalmist in Psalm 23:

> The LORD is my shepherd, I shall not be in want. He makes me lie down in green pastures, he leads me beside quiet waters, he restores my soul. He guides me in paths of righteousness for his name's sake. Even though I walk through the valley of the shadow of death, I will fear no evil, for you are with me; your rod and your staff comfort me. You prepare a table before me in the presence of my enemies. You anoint my head with oil; my cup overflows. Surely goodness and love will follow me all the days of my life, and I will dwell in the house of the LORD forever.

The lake, the trees, and the animals seemed to call me to peace. Shells on the beach reminded me of home. The colors were so similar. I picked up a couple of peach and ice blue swirled ones which were as big as my fist. The symmetry of the houses of these living things was so like those from my boyhood in Florida where I often walked alone and meditated on life.

Birds and small animals came to the water to drink. We all shared a common bond as living things. A time of ecstasy that was. With a sense of reverence, I invaded quietly and humbly that naked beauty. In spite of my loneliness and amnesia, I had a forceful sense that my presence there was no accident and that in the end good would come of it.

I began to feel less alone. Hope for seeing my family and friends again soon grew with each passing hour. My resolve increased to not only survive but to be ready to return to and defend those whom I loved. Somehow the Creator knew I was there, and he knew me. And I knew him.

What was and is his relationship with the creatures of this world? Are they creatures mostly like humans? Do they sense him as we do, some knowing him and others denying him? I feel at peace that he knows, and for now, I do not need to know. It will be seen in his timing. I will seek him as best I know. My current walk with the Creator is enough at this moment and at this time.

Back at the camp site, I read the Bible again for some time. I read of Gideon and his 300 soldiers defeating a larger army. I marveled at the strength of Samson. Cold chills ran over me when I read how he killed more in death than in life, as I wondered if this may someday apply to me. I felt a oneness with Nehemiah as he rebuilt the walls of Jerusalem to protect his kin from enemies. I was awed by the power unleashed by Elijah and Elisha as they served God. Esther took her life into her hands to see an enemy of her people thwarted and removed. On and on, God's people won against incredible odds because they served the Creator.

On the other hand, the stories of those who served and were not victorious in this life were sobering. I did not want to think about them for long. The similarities to my situation were too unsettling.

As I finished reading, darkness approached. Without understanding the details, I felt a deep and peaceful sense of immediate purpose. A hymn of praise came to my lips, and I sang it softly beside the quiet lake and glowing embers of the dwindling fire. The birds stopped their calling and listened to this strange song from a tongue alien to their world, as if giving me my turn to solo during their symphony. After the song, all remained quiet. Warm tears carved wet trails down my cheeks. Memories of past simple times of precious fellowship with friends were parading through my very heart.

I bedded down in my shelter for the night. The evening was bursting with love and power. A beautiful and delicate symphony was playing. The sound was not heard, but the touch on the heart was felt deeply. As if a child again, I felt strong and warm arms surround me and carry me gently into rest.

The next morning, I awakened refreshed and strong, ready for new adventures after my own Lohana. A full breakfast beside the campfire satisfied. I had relocated some of the drones from the cities to locations between them, set to record sounds of horns, speech, and of human-like movements. I checked their recordings one by one and focused on the snippets of conversations. The Makurani were back on my trail in large numbers after Lohana, and the Kamikini were still enjoying their peaceful lives. The Makurani signals from the field were strong near my main shelter, so I took warning to be watchful as I went back there. After packing all the gear and some food left over, I put out the fire, loaded myself onto the lifter, and headed back.

Along the way I picked out a target occasionally to test out my weapons while flying. After about an hour of playing I was able to split a small boulder with laser cannons using either hand. They worked well off the energy generator and did not affect flying power in the bursts of several seconds I used. The scope rifle was not as effective while in motion, but it worked well when I stopped in midair. The virtual absence of wind was an exceptional help.

During the early morning hours of the flight I also tested out a computer enhanced visor assembly which worked with the helmet. The assembly included enemy tracking and infrared viewing. By computer enhancements I could aim a low level of laser beam from the cannon at a target to sight it in, then fire a strong burst of beam using thought commands and the visor. This was more fun than the multi-sensory video screen games I played as a youngster. But this time I had an underlying feeling of seriousness in the play.

As I approached the shelter site I came in low and slow. All looked okay as the shelter area came into view. The Makurani had been alarmingly close to the shelter site, and there were no horn signals for over an hour, so I was wary. As I hovered a yard above the ground near the site, I felt a thud in my front pack.

An arrow! Another struck my backpack. I immediately issued the thought command, "Emergency rise now!" The lifter accelerated straight up and slowed to 2,500 feet as a preset height. My ears were killing me. I forgot to wear protectors for that. I won't forget again!

I came back down to 200 feet, and my ears were better. Seeing me hovering there, several Makurani tried to hit me with their crossbow arrows. A few rose to my altitude but not with any momentum left. One or two hit me and fell back down. I used the scope rifle to pick off 12 exposed soldiers in rapid succession.

The rest of the soldiers, if any, lay low. My gear started picking up sounds and images of frantic movements in the underbrush. It then targeted their movements, and one by one I was able to target and hit them with bullets. I then swung out of the clearing into the trees to come around behind the bugler who had started blowing signals. Looking through the scope, I found him at 500 feet away. When I got closer, I took out the squadron leader using it, along with his two assistants.

For the next half hour, I played "cat and mouse" at 50-150 feet up. I was a powerful mouse, and they were the cats who could not resist a good target. Apparently, they felt my defeat was critically important to their people. After I had killed another 15 archers, the new field leader ordered a retreat on his horn. He signaled that they were to regroup and attack again in coordinated fashion if I was willing to continue playing this game.

I retired momentarily to check where two arrows had bruised me, and one had lodged a half-inch into my left thigh. I dislodged it and used the small first aid kit to stop the bleeding until I could get back to my healing robot. *A little pain will not stop me now.*

The competitive fever was high. Maurice often complained about it on earth. He said it would drive me to greatness or death, and maybe both at the same time. The first part was fine by me, but the second part could wait awhile. At least until I was a great grandfather.

I discovered where the soldiers were regrouping. Timing their jog time and reloading the rifle, I moved into position nearby. Hovering at 25 feet above the ground, I looked through the trees and caught them in my scope at close to 500 feet away in a small clearing on this side of a lake. About 20 soldiers were meeting to discuss their new plans.

Moving at 10 mph toward them I began to pick them off quickly with the rifle, aiming from right to left. A few scrambled to the left, and I got all but one as they ran frantically away. I chased the last one into the trees. He saw me and turned quickly to fire his crossbow. As the arrow flew, I hit him squarely and saw him start to fall as the arrow struck my upper left arm.

When it plunged deep into the biceps muscle, my head jerked back as I screamed in pain. I stopped the lifter and went up through the tree limbs which brushed against me to over 300 feet and applied first aid. I carefully excised the arrow and stopped the bleeding.

I went back down and checked on each soldier where he fell. This platoon had 50 soldiers whom I had killed. I was not sure what I would do if one had lived and tried to surrender. Again, some died of wounds that looked minor.

The adrenalin rush was starting to make me feel lightheaded. Using deep breathing to calm down, I went carefully to the shelter site and got all my gear. Tying them to the back of the sky lifter, I flew off a few miles and landed to drop them off and use the healing robot. An hour later, my wounds were healed. The blood loss was slight but coming down from the adrenaline rush was hard.

I was still wary of the possibility that other soldiers might be near. Remounting the lifter, I flew up into a tall tree to take a breather. Soon I was napping for an hour. I awakened stiff yet feeling better.

I flew down and drank freely of the water in the river lake there and ate some food from the pack. The food tasted like cardboard after the excitement, and I was trembling a little and forcing myself to eat.

After a few minutes of walking around and gathering my emotions and wits about me, I flew cautiously back to the new site. The drone transmissions from Hekanalo mentioned the attack. The nearest troops were an hour away and were ordered to go to the spot. I checked for any equipment I may have left back there and find none was missing.

I picked up the shelter gear at the temporary spot to the south and carried it with the lifter to a beautiful site I saw about 25 miles south and a little east of Kohilo. I found an overhang near the top of a cliff 500 feet high with a captivating view of the northern scenery. Sunsets and sunrises would be gorgeous from there. The cliff was shaped like a one mile long concave crescent facing north. My new shelter was at the eastern side. A small waterfall plummeted over the cliff at the western edge. The ice blue water splashed onto coral rocks below into a gathering pond and flowed as a narrow river to the north, nourishing the forests and fields along the way.

I wished I could share that beauty with my family and friends. *Maurice would love this place for a weekend retreat. Michelle and the teens would laugh and frolic in the waterfall and pond below.* In beautiful places such as this, Maurice and I would often talk of world events on Earth and plan our future work. "Maybe someday", I sighed. The sense of mission inside me remained high in contrast to the natural beauty.

I settled in by digging out a bigger shelf on which to live under the overhang. Going to the bottom of the cliff, I gathered wild berries and fruit. Some wild vegetables were also scattered about in small quantities. After stocking up and eating a full meal without a fire, I sat and watched the day end while musing about life and death and strange worlds.

I was sobered by the fact that the Makurani were intent on killing me. Any hope of approaching them in peace was evaporated. They had attacked me three times, and 77 of them were dead. What a contrast there was between their hatred of me and the peace of that place!

I remembered times spent fishing and hunting with Dad and Grandpa. How I wished for those times now! We talked of life, God, nature, and anything my little inquisitive mind wanted to discuss. I shared how I wanted to help others, to "benefit mankind". When younger, I hated to put worms on the hooks. It did not feel right to see the little creatures squirm in death to catch another creature to kill for us to eat and live. The whole idea seemed so horrific. Dad would talk to me about it. He understood and did not laugh at me or put me down.

Heaviness of sleep came and sat beside me. I felt very lonely again. The covers I pulled around me helped somewhat. I nodded off as a wet tear wound its way slowly down my cheek and for a time washed away my loneliness in waves of sleep.

Chapter 8: Encounters Day and Night

I slept soundly that night, only stirring occasionally. Just after dawn, a sound near my shelter awakened me with a start. A small avalanche of pebbles fell near me at the front of the overhang. It came from directly overhead.

I was facing north lying on my right side. Moved by stark fear and groggy from sudden awakening, I reached for the laser cannon and energy generator at my left side. I quickly put on them and then the helmet and infrared visor. The sounds moved to the left as I faced out of the shelter, my right arm aiming that way to destroy whatever threatened me. A shape began to appear there at my level. Coming into full view was a large mammal like creature which was as tall as a giraffe but looked like a skinny elephant with longer neck and medium-length trunk. It was marked like a zebra with brown lines on a tan body.

The creature moved without hurry and gracefully to the front of the shelter. Ready to fire, I watched its every move. It sniffed around at the left front and found my food supply. It looked briefly at me, checked the food, then kneeled down and began to eat. After it ate for a while, I scooted over near the food. I cautiously picked a piece of food out of the pile with my left arm, aiming still with my right. The creature continued to eat casually as I brought the food to my mouth. It seemed unafraid and willing to share.

The creature appeared to be an herbivore. I watched it leisurely eat and remembered the birds and small animals I had seen the last few days. None of them seemed afraid of me. At times flocks of birds had followed me around when I walked along the ground. The Ontarions apparently do not eat animals, but exist on vegetables, berries, and fruits. I was glad I did not shoot any animals for food and thus ruin this world

47

so nonviolent in its ecology. How ironic that the speaking creatures pose such a threat to me, and me to some of them.

When the serene beast finished its meal, it rose to its feet and reached out its trunk toward me. I touched it with my left hand, and it snorted with delight. Then it turned and sauntered slowly down the hill. Soon I saw it eating from berry bushes and reaching up in the tall trees to pick the better fruits.

I was on friendly terms with nature and the animals, hunted by the Makurani, and separated from the Kamikini who I remember as present when my trauma occurred. I believed it was time to meet some Kamikini. My plan to meet them was ready, and I continued to be wary of the Makurani.

After a breakfast in the field of wild berries and fruits, I packed up a few items to take to Kohilo. Flying off at moderate speed, I swung to the southwest of the city and set down. I then used a drone to fly over their city at 50 feet and act as a loudspeaker to transmit in their native tongue.

"This is the creature from Earth seeking to talk to a Kamikini elder. Please respond." I heard excited actions, then repeated my message.

I saw a man come to below the drone and look up at it, saying, "This is Captain Hawiki. You may speak to me."

"Have you known an Earth creature who visited your city?"

"I have seen him and know of him. Only Generals Leahu and Maniho of the military have been with him for any time."

"Let me speak to one of them here in the open. I am that creature."

"I will inform them immediately. Please wait."

I waited for what felt like an hour but was only five minutes. Then someone came to the drone site and spoke up to it, "This is General Maniho. Earth creature, please give your name."

"I am Daniel. Complete my name."

"You are then Daniel Wayne Davidson. You spent five days with us here in Kohilo. We each learned a little of each other's speech. (He paused.) We do not understand why you screamed and ran away when you looked at the glass screen."

So, he was there during the incident that caused my severe trauma. "I do not know. Perhaps you can help me to remember. There is much to discuss."

"Yes, there is. Please bring your strange bird down here to make it easier to talk."

I moved the drone down to hover at 5 feet above the ground and 10 feet in front of him.

He continued, "Will you come now to meet us? We have heard of your battles with the Makurani. Can we trust you? You locked General Leahu and me in your control room and ran away."

"You can trust me. Right now, I am not sure who it is that I myself can trust. The Makurani have attacked me three times. I am being extremely careful."

"Come back to Kohilo and we will talk."

"I cannot. If you will trust me, I will tell you where to meet me."

After a few seconds pause, General Maniho spoke, "I will come as you wish. My advisors want me not to meet you, but I will."

"I appreciate your willingness to meet me."

I then described to him the place I had prepared for the meeting. It was about 5 miles from Kohilo, on the side opposite the way to Hekanalo. He agreed to meet me in about 5 hours, alone except for a bodyguard of three men. I advised him to bring ten men. I was not threatened, but there may be Makurani about. He said three would do. We courteously bid each other well and signed off. I flew the drone on to the meeting site and perched it in a tree.

I flew immediately to the spot to make final preparations for the meeting. I was very paranoid at this point and wanted any advantage to protect my life. After a couple of hours arranging and checking on the equipment I brought, I felt it was ready. I then flew back to my new main shelter and got prepared for this special moment.

I felt so excited I could hardly eat lunch. On one hand, this felt like the first time I asked a girl out for a date. On the other, it reminded me of the tension I had before major sports events in college. In case there was a battle, I wanted to adequately fill up, especially with water. I also felt apprehension and inadequacy. My concern was that my heightened state of anxiety might dull my senses. To avoid letting my emotions take over and leave me too vulnerable, I ask the ewallet to lead me through a preparation checklist. It suggested I consider the plastic suit armor along with the helmet and visor.

Of course! Maurice used to say I was a little foolhardy when in competition and should protect myself more. He was a world class chess player when in his twenties. I could beat him on occasion now, and he said I would be among the world's greatest players if I learned to protect my king better. This was one time when I remembered to do so. Like the lifter, it was designed to enfold me automatically, so I had it on in less than 20 seconds. It was shaped to my clothed body and looked almost transparent.

After a prayer for safety, I set out for the meeting site in the lifter. I took the scope rifle, a laser cannon, the weaponized shoulder pads, and a pistol with silencer. I also took a Makurani horn, sword, shield, and a crossbow with ten arrows. I arrived an hour before the scheduled meeting time.

From one mile out I circled the site above the trees in a decreasing spiral, looking for suspicious signs of military action. Seeing none, I settled off to the side of the clearing where we would meet. I then checked my drone transmissions for signs of nearby activity and used an audio enhancer to listen around me.

After another 20 minutes, I heard sounds from the direction of Kohilo. The general and his aides were approaching the site. I sent a drone to hover before them and advise that I was there and waiting. So far, I had heard no unusual activity from the drones that would indicate any Makurani were in the area.

He and three aides entered the edge of the clearing. I had stored my equipment in the trees except for the lifter. I floated out slowly to meet them. The general crossed his wrists with open hands in greeting. His aides stood behind him. None appeared to have weapons except small knives at their waists. I had brought only the pistol in a belt pack. I crossed my wrists and set down a few yards away.

"General, please walk over to me without your aides."

He came over slowly and gracefully, a strong looking Ontarian over six feet tall, dressed in full field uniform. In flowing and resonant Ontarion speech, he said, "Hail, Daniel. We meet again. How have you been? We have had distress about you since you left that day. We have also heard the Makurani have attacked you and lost each time, as you also said happened. I delight to see you looking well, yet you look tired."

He was right. Several days on my own fearing for my life had left me exhausted. "I took a Lohana. You should have seen me before that." I laughed.

He smiled. "I remember your humor. We are less able to see the humorous unless it is quite strong. You are able to enjoy the simpler pleasures better than we are."

He continued, "And what is this I see on you? It looks like a clear membrane about you."

"General, I come for a purpose which is profoundly serious to me. I am wearing a type of protection over my body, because I still do not remember you. Can we talk freely?"

"I have always talked freely with you. I have not changed."

"Maybe so, but I have. Something happened in Kohilo when I was looking at the screen which caused me severe emotional trauma. Some of my memory is blocked. I do not remember you at this time. I need your help to remember what happened up until then. Even now I am somewhat afraid of you and any other Ontarion. My electronic wallet has told me the Kamikini are my reason for being here."

At this, he paused. Then he said very deliberately, "You never told us why you were here before you ran away. But we believe you are the Hakani. Are you truly the Hakani?"

"I do not know about Hakani. I only know I need to talk to you to recover my memory. Will you help me?"

"Certainly. How can I help? What do you desire to know right now?"

I asked him to wait briefly as I put the lifter off nearby, then we sat down in the grass. For the next half hour, we talked about how they met me and what we did in Kohilo. I had him start at the beginning and go forward. A couple of times it got intense for me, so I asked him to wait until I was calmer before going on.

He said I had arrived in a large spherical ball about 3 miles north of Kohilo. As I was making my way toward Kohilo, two of their soldiers had happened upon me about a mile out. They were frightened, but I indicated no harm and spoke a few words of Ontarion. I appeared to be in great pain, so they brought me back in a stretcher to Kohilo while other soldiers brought my sphere and gear to a place inside the city. The sphere could be carried by six soldiers when empty of loose equipment.

I apparently used my healing kit to cure whatever caused the excruciating pain. After using my healing kit and sleeping for nearly ten hours overnight, I met him and General Leahu. They were fascinated by my advanced tools and equipment. They also seemed more impressed by the fact that I came from another world. For that day, I worked at learning more of their language as they showed me many things in the city. I also noticed they were reluctant to have me step outside the city walls. I slept in a room at his residence that night.

The next day they introduced me to a few people in the government. At the day's end, they gave me a better bedroom in the residence and a room to set up my equipment nearby. They also advised me to put locks on the doors to the jump vehicle and my room of equipment. We talked each day at length, and I showed them some of my equipment. So impressive! On the fourth day, I spent the day in the equipment room working diligently on something. He had become my main contact at that point.

On the morning of day five, I told him to bring General Leahu and come to the equipment room after lunch. There I had set up several electronic gadgets and put a large flat screen in the middle. I acted like I was delighted. As they watched, changing shapes came on the screen, and they heard voices. What incredible powers! In this temperate world they had no need for energy sources except for cooking, so this looked like miracles from God to them. I talked to the screen shapes, and they seemed to talk back in human language.

At first, they seemed to delight me, then I started yelling and screaming. For a few minutes, I did things with the screen, ignoring their presence. I became very loud and upset.

Finally, the screen showed a solid pattern, and I appeared to be so upset that I backed away from the screen, grabbed my head, and loudly yelled, "No! No! No!" I did this over and over. He and Leahu were shocked. When I kept on, they decided to try and comfort me. When they did, I looked strangely wild and pushed them away. Then I fled out the door and locked them in.

When they were taken out a few minutes later by junior soldiers who had the extra keys I left them, they heard I had fled the residence. They sent soldiers to search for me, but no one could find me.

He finished by saying, "The Makurani had already found out you had been there, and we were very afraid they would kill you before you could come back to our people. The Makurani questioned us severely about you, and we told what we knew. Although the Makurani had many scout teams looking for you, we prayed strongly that you would be safe."

"We had soldiers going out to look for you, and we hoped you would see them and make contact. I became more concerned each day you stayed away. When you finally contacted us, we celebrated. You do not know how glad I am to talk to you again."

I looked away into the woods for a while. Then I turned and peered deeply into his eyes and asked, "What did I see on the screen?"

"We do not know. Such shapes were new to us. They were changing rapidly, and we could not understand them."

"What the screen showed were images from Earth. I fear something terrible has happened to my family and friends there. My ewallet told me my mission was to come here and help you defeat the Makurani and bring my family here to live. If they have been taken and killed, then I am alone, and my mission is in vain."

At this, he appeared shocked, and I become overcome with anger and hurt. I get up and walked away to let myself cry for a time, sometimes letting out a growling breath and tightening the muscles in my arms and fists to release my anger. Maniho, as he let me call him, sat by respectfully.

When I sat back down, he reached out to touch my sleeve and acted startled by the feel of the plastic armor. I removed my right glove and touched his hand with mine.

I offered, "I appreciate your concern for me. Please forgive me if I wear this special type of armor for a while longer. I am still uneasy about trusting anyone."

Then I proposed as I put the glove back on, "Maniho, I need to stand and walk around a bit before we talk further. Will you walk with me?"

"Certainly. There is a lake with a small stream over there. We could walk there for a drink and return if you wish."

We walked to the edge of the clearing together. He instructed his aides to follow at a distance. At a few yards into the trees, I felt my armor stop a fast object on the chest plate. An arrow from a crossbow fell to the ground. Another struck my waist and fell the same way. Maniho yelled, "Makurani!"

I pulled out the pistol and shot each Makurani I saw. We both ran back to the clearing. His aides came to his side immediately and surrounded him, then they dove for ground cover.

Quickly I ran back and put on my lifter and armed the weapons on it. As I ascended, I saw Makurani soldiers shooting arrows at Maniho and his aides. They were helpless against them. My first thoughts were to protect Maniho and his aides.

Some Makurani had run past the Kamikini and were headed toward me screaming and firing arrows. I moved toward them and easily took out each as I flew toward my only Ontarion friend. Several arrows with lethal aim bounced harmlessly off me. The Makurani who shot them had a moment of shock on their faces at their bouncing off, then the shock of sudden death.

Within a minute after the first arrow flew, I was at the side of Maniho and his aides. Allowing all of the Makurani to get into the clearing, I picked them off as I saw them. Then by voice commands I activated the trap I had set, which was to destroy any Ontarion more than 25 feet away from me. An automated laser cannon and a semi-automatic dart gun placed on opposite sides of the clearing had sensors to detect moving objects. These soon finished off the contingent of enemy soldiers. The few who were too close to me were quickly dispatched by my pistol. In the distance, a horn sounded, sending word about their attack and defeat.

I turned off the automatic weapons in the trap and looked at the Kamikini at my feet. The three aides had used their bodies to shield the general and were dead from several arrows each. Maniho was underneath. I carefully pulled the aides off and found he had taken an arrow in the back of his right shoulder. As I used my first aid kit, he said before he passed out, "Poison."

I picked him up in my arms, tied him to me, and flew quickly to my new main shelter. I threw off the lifter and used the healing robot immediately. He was barely alive. I showed an arrow to the robot, then let it examine him to set up for his slightly different body chemistry. The robot made some adjustments for his body and began to neutralize the poison which it discovered on the arrow. In a brief time, his condition improved, and the healing robot declared that he should be okay after some sleep. Much relieved, I covered him up away from the entrance and went back to the meeting site to clean up.

A contingent of 125 soldiers had attacked us on the run, hearing that General Maniho had left the city with his aides and headed west. I flew briefly to Kohilo to tell them what had happened. They said they would handle burial actions as soon as they got to the meeting site. I said I would bring the general from my secret shelter as soon as he was able, but I would call in occasionally via drone. Flying back to the clearing, I dismantled the trap equipment, then took it all back to the shelter.

Maniho was still sleeping. The healing robot said he should sleep overnight and awaken late next morning.

I ate a simple meal and gave thanks for my life and his as the twin suns were setting. For all I knew, he and General Leahu might be my only friends in the entire Universe. His body was resting peacefully as I anxiously awaited having another opportunity to talk with him.

That night, I was so angry I could not go to sleep for a long time. I sat in my armor propped up in front of Maniho with the scope rifle and pistol in my hands and infrared visor on my face. *No one will get me or my friend tonight!*

Chapter 9: Ontario's History

As dawn broke, I awoke to the familiar morning songs of birds and small animals as they went about eating berries and fruits. They sing with a richer mixture of tones than on earth for a beautiful symphony of peace and joy.

General Maniho was fast asleep. He looked peaceful and strong, yet somehow childlike. He gave the impression of trust, as a youngster at home in its own bed.

I checked the drone transmissions for Makurani conversations. The conversations showed they had not discovered my latest hideout, and they were fiercely angry at me and the Kamikini. After I finished listening and went to the front of the shelter, I uttered a short burst of praise to the Creator for this natural beauty all around. Then I shed my armor and most of my clothes and joined the animals in gathering breakfast.

I felt a harmony with the natural surroundings which surprised me. There was much that felt like Home. The green trees, the dark tree bark, the many pastel colors of the flowers and bushes. The many bright fruits and berries. The azure blue of the sky. The shallow angle of the suns, so that the day always appeared to be no older than mid-morning or younger than midafternoon. Rapturous beauty. The kind that brought men and women out in droves to hunt and fish on Earth. And there I waded in it waist deep, partaking of it as I went.

I brought an armful of food back to the shelter for Maniho to eat later. At a nearby stream, I cleaned my clothes which were soiled. Afterward, I enjoyed a swim in the clear water. I shaved off several days of beard and brushed my teeth. A little shampoo, and I felt like a new man. At the shelter, I put on clean clothes and cleaned my gear. Having a guest made me conscious to look my best. I also felt less lonely with Maniho there beside me.

At around noon, Maniho awakened. He came around slowly, eating a little food I handed him and looking out of the shelter while lying down. After he sat up, he took deep drinks of water and closed his eyes to relax. He felt with his left hand where the arrow had been, then smiled at me with a smile which grew as I looked at him.

He stood and stretched, then said in Ontarian, "I thought I would not awaken in Ontario, but here I am. believe we were taking a walk before all of this. How about one now?"

"Certainly. Are you able to talk, or shall we wait?"

He replied as he walked out of the shelter, "I am able to walk and talk, although I feel sluggish. I feel fine otherwise after that ordeal. What did you do to me?"

"I used my healing machine on you. The machine identified the poison and neutralized it. I told your soldiers in Kohilo I was bringing you here and would bring you back when well."

"My thanks, Daniel. No one has ever survived a Makurani arrow before now."

"Strange. I have been struck twice and lived without problems. That which is poison to you must not be to me."

He looked at me soberly as I spoke and now looked straight ahead. He asked softly, "What of my aides?"

"They were killed protecting you. I destroyed the enemy soldiers but not before your aides were shot several times before I could get all of you out of there. I am sorry I could not save them."

He was visibly moved. "There were too many. Besides, you were the one they were after. We were targets only because we were with you. You have honored us by allowing us to be so casual with you in your presence."

He paused. Then looking straight into my eyes, he said, "I know now that which we have only hoped is true. You are certainly the Hakani."

At that point, this graceful creature stopped and bowed low before me. I was stunned and said in my embarrassment, "Do not bow to me. I am a creature even as you are. Please stand up."

He stood at my insistence, but a fresh look of reverence and awe were in his eyes and face. "My eyes have seen Hakani, and he has rescued me. How soon will you at last save all the Kamikini?"

I looked him straight in the eyes then walked away to think for a moment. *What is this? I have chills again. Have I stumbled into a prophetic expectation of this people? This is too awesome.*

I needed to know more. I walked back slowly, then asked, "Who is this Hakani?"

"Hakani is our expected rescuer, the one who will avenge us on the Makurani and bring us into the final era of peace. In the final era, we expand into final union with Ahueha to be in his realm forever. The enemies of the Kamikini will be no more. So Ahueha promised us by Anakela 40 years ago."

"Is Ahueha the Creator?"

Serenely he answered, "He is more than Creator. The name we know him by means Creator Sustainer-Father-Mother."

"Please tell me more about the Anakela and 40 years ago."

"At that time, we had women and children. The Makurani and the Kamikini were the last of a once great race which inhabited this planet. The Creator made the first two of our kind over 300,000 years ago to mature and then be his servants in his own realm. Such is the final destiny for each of us."

"We live here as you have seen. As each of us grew into maturity, he or she at a late stage would begin to softly glow from within as if they were a candle in a jar. When looking at them, one would see that they also seemed to have a faint light shining from behind him or her. By a few months after that, the newly glorified one, or Anakela, would have become transformed and without sexuality. In a final beautiful ceremony, the new Anakela would bring friends together and bid farewell. Then a door would open in space. The glorified one would step through the door and disappear from view into Ahueha's realm as the door closed.

At times, we would see such a one again to bring special words to us. Some words were of joy and some were of sorrow."

"Our records tell us nearly half of the Anakelani turned against Ahueha and fell from their glory back to here around 10,000 years ago. A vague reference said most went to another place where we cannot go. There we are told Ahueha battles them now, and we have battled the ones here. The Makurani are the last of the ones thrown back to Ontario. We Kamikini are the last of the ones not yet glorified."

"We supposedly could have made the mighty weapons you have. Ahueha took away our understanding of such things so the Makurani could not use them to destroy us. As you see, our weapons are simple."

"We and the Makurani have dwindled down after much warfare to one final city each. An Anakela came from Ahueha some fifty years ago to tell us the final era was almost here. We must no longer defend ourselves from the Makurani. Carry weapons, but do not defend. We were to trust completely in Ahueha. After this one left, it was only a few months before the Makurani knew of it. They came and taunted us. Before our eyes, they slaughtered our women and children cruelly and unmercifully. Each of us was forced to watch them die in pain. They decided to let us live, so they could see us go on without them and continually remind us of our cowardice and grief."

"They want us to fight them, for they know we cannot win. Ahueha will not support us. And since we will not fight them, they make us bring them food every day, while they practice their military arts and skills. You may have noticed our several caravans going there and back each day. That is probably the main reason they have not already killed us. We are of some value to them while we are alive, and none if dead."

I broke in. "How have you been able to live until now? How could you stand to let the Makurani go unavenged all this time?"

"After the women and children were killed, we wept for days and weeks. We cried out to Ahueha in our pain. We could not understand his way in this. This was too overwhelming. We could not bear it. Three months after the slaughter, we were all meeting in the central square. General Leahu and I were, and are still, the co-leaders of the Kamikini. We called for four hours of prayer in the square every night, starting four hours before sunset. On one particular night, a bright light came from the sky as we were nearly finished and settled in front of us. A door opened in space and a creature stepped through. It was the Anakela who had spoken ten years earlier."

"This one told us our women and children were with Ahueha and gave each of us a glimpse at his family with Ahueha. Before each one of us a window opened into that realm. We could see them living happily with him. The Makurani gave us last memories of their pain. Now we had new visions of their peace. We were overjoyed and deeply thankful."

"That Anakela also gave a message of hope. 'Today Hakani is born in another world. He will come to you and be your avenger on the Makurani. You must not lay a hand on a Makurani to hurt him until Hakani comes and even after he comes. Only Hakani may destroy the Makurani, and he will utterly destroy them all. Then you will each continue becoming glorified and join your families with Ahueha. If a Makurani kills you before then, you will be glorified suddenly in that realm if you give no defense.'"

"'This planet will die ten years after Hakani comes. All races in this realm will end. All Kamikini will have been made perfect.'"

Sobered but curious, I asked him when the visitation had been. He told me the date. Then he told how their calendar works and I fed the data into my ewallet.

I asked him, "What makes you think I am Hakani?"

"The time for Hakani to appear is at hand. You are not of our world. You have many superior weapons. Our poisons do not harm you. You killed many Makurani already, and they seek your life. You are most certainly Hakani."

We walked back to the shelter in silence. He was in expectant awe, and I was in shock. *A scientist engineer on earth becomes a mass killer on another world? A Christian who loves science and wants to walk with God destroys an entire race? How can this be?*

And yet my being there aligned with the prophecies. On the other hand, what if it was only an elaborate trick? And if this was a trick, what was its purpose? A lot of caution seemed in order.

"Do you have records of the visit which told of Hakani?"

"Yes, in my residence. Would you like to see them?"

"Yes. Maniho, this all comes as a shock to me. I need some more evidence. I am sure I was not sent here with such a great purpose in mind." (Although I still could not fully remember.)

"Then let us go back to Kohilo. There you can see our writings and the room with your things. Perhaps then you will remember all you must know."

I asked him to stay with me one more night to allow me to think and ponder these things. He agreed, so we spent the rest of the day talking of this planet and their history, including stories about his families and friends such as Leahu. I also told him of Earth and its history. He was fascinated by the biblical accounts, especially those about one-third of the angels falling from heaven. The stories of Christ were hardly believable. To think that Ahueha would become human! I told him I would fill him in on present times when my memory returned.

I also asked him to describe the family life of the Kamikini before the great slaughter. He said the women were equal partners with them, and they were very affectionate and supportive. Normally, they were naturally in agreement on all aspects of their married life. If they ever differed on anything they could not resolve themselves, then they consulted both sets of parents (if not already glorified). If this resulted in an impasse, then they consulted the elders, a panel of three women and three men in each city. If the elders were not in consensus, then they all prayed and fasted until Ahueha revealed his will. In all things, they obeyed Ahueha gladly.

Childrearing was a joy. The women bore them seven months after conception without pain and struggle. The children were naturally obedient and grew to full height and adulthood by age 12. They were not consumed by lust, and so premarital affairs were a non-issue. At age 16, they were married to someone they were drawn to by Ahueha.

I decided not to tell him how it was on Earth. The human race was so far from ideal that I felt he would only be shocked and horrified.

Toward sunset, we were feeling it was time for sleep. It came slowly but deeply to each of us. Again, I slept in armor.

Later in the night I awakened with all of this news running through my restless mind. Using the data fed into the electronic wallet earlier, I had it calculate the date on earth when the Anakela said Hakani was born in another place. It matched the exact day when I was born in Tampa, Florida. After that, I lay awake for a long time before sleep came again.

The next morning Maniho and I both wanted to get to Kohilo. I gathered up all my gear in the shelter and attached it to me and to Maniho. I strapped him to my front on the lifter, sitting on my footrest just inside the windshield to keep us balanced and my view unhindered.

I wanted him to wear my extra armor suit, but he insisted on going as he was. Soon we were traveling at 1,000 feet and 60 mph toward Kohilo.

When we got to Kohilo, I swooped down to float over the city walls and taller buildings and then moved slowly over the city. Maniho motioned toward the central square and I aimed us for it. We floated over the dwellings on the edge of the square and the open place came slowly into view. As we came in over the dwellings, a large crowd was revealed to be waiting in the square.

The moment was pregnant with anticipation. I had both the desire to fly away from there and the desire to continue. Yet Maniho was calm and expectant, like someone going toward a Sunday picnic. In the strength of his peace, I moved on into the city.

Chapter 10: Hakani in Kohilo

At the sight of us, they knelt on the ground and bowed down. Moving on over the walls, we came down into the square at Kohilo. When we sat down in the middle of them, the silence was so thick I could hear myself breathing. Maniho untied his straps and stood up as I untied myself from the lifter, looking around the whole time.

He gave a command and two soldiers came at once and helped me remove my packs and gear. Then they took their place again in the crowd.

Maniho then told me, "All 3,078 Kamikini are here to greet you. They too now believe you are Hakani. Please greet my people."

After a deep breath, I spoke these words in their language, "People of Kohilo, I do not know whether I am this Hakani you look for. I only know I came from another world to help you and to help my family back on my world. I desire your peace in this world. General Maniho has told me much. I must learn more before I can finish my mission. Please treat me as you would any other Kamiki. My name is Daniel. Pray for me. I need your help."

General Maniho then spoke to them, "Friends, we have come to believe this is the one, although he has not personally received such a word about himself. He has asked to study to see if these things are true. We will allow him full freedom in and about our city. Please help him in any way he asks you. You may now go back to your duties."

General Leahu then came forward and greeted us both. They escorted me into the residence where they both lived. Soldiers brought my gear and the lifter along.

Soon they showed me the guest room where I had fled from. We put the gear there and went for a walk inside the leaders' residence. After that we sat down in a spacious hall to talk and have the midday meal.

Maniho did most of the talking. Leahu was cordial but reserved. He had what looked like dim light radiating from his skin, had long blond hair falling down to his shoulders, and seemed to be very much at peace. I asked about Leahu's different appearance.

Maniho explained, "Leahu is now our oldest Kamiki and is beginning the glorification process. His personality is becoming gentler and more in tune with Ahueha. Because of this, many of the daily leadership duties fall to me as next in command. He is our leader in spiritual areas, and I lead in the practical areas of day to day life on Ontario."

Turning to Leahu, I asked, "Does Ahueha tell you about me?"

Leahu answered, "He speaks to me about many things in many areas. Yet he hides from me any word I have asked him about you. I can only walk by his former revelations."

"What sorts of things does he talk to you about?" I asked.

"He speaks mainly to me about individual Kamikini, about his desires for them. Occasionally, he will tell me about major events which are coming. But about this most critical area he will say nothing, although I have pled with tears. Nevertheless, my prayers always include requests for your safety, and that you may fulfill his desire for you here."

Turning to Maniho, I asked, "What do you suppose the Makurani are doing now? Surely they know I am here."

He answered, "We also believe they know of your presence here today. No doubt they saw us come in today. My guess is that they are deciding how best to attack you next. Yet we have seen no unusual activity outside the city so far."

After the meal, Maniho said, "Are you ready to look again at the equipment room?"

After a deep sigh and a glance at them both, I replied, "Yes, I am ready. I feel a sense of urgency. I hope I will be able to deal with what I have left behind me there."

In a few minutes, we arrived with several helpers at the equipment room. I looked around at the sending and receiving television equipment in front of us. It was exactly as I remembered it in my first image after the amnesia. As they watched, I turned on each piece of equipment and adjusted its settings. I stood back and watched the assembly hum. The screen had a dark, blank surface reflecting my face. A rugged but cautious man looked at me from the screen, a look of fierceness on his face.

I was lost in a blank stare for a moment, then I began to interact with the monitor controls to see if any signals could be detected. No television signals of any type were in the air. I checked the recording system and found nearly two hours of received signals that were recorded.

I asked Maniho and Leahu to sit beside me as I prepared the recording. I told them, "If I scream again, please hold me down and have me stop the recording. Hold me in your arms and hug me close to let me know I am not alone. Do not let me run away again."

They agreed solemnly. We sat close in the knee chairs of this world, with me in the center between these two tall, lean soldiers.

I started the recording. It began with Maurice trying to tune in to my signal and vice versa. I could hear my voice while watching and hearing him. Behind him were my wife and children. Sometimes they came closer to talk to me. Off to the right rear was the other spherical jump machine about 15 feet in diameter.

"Is that like my sphere?", I asked the generals. They were not familiar with such images, but as I showed them what was on the screen they began to understand. They apparently did not understand what they saw a few days ago, either.

"Yes," They say. "Your machine which is in the large storage room nearby looks like that."

"I must see it later then. For now, please continue to watch with me. I want to recover my memory.... I want to be .... whole again." I felt I needed to say this, as much for me as for them.

After rewinding it, we saw Maurice was speaking happily like a little boy with a new toy. He and my family were happy to see I arrived safely. Maurice spoke with joy about how our computations on space interconnections proved true, and now the first human has bridged the gap.

I explained how I arrived in pain. It took the Kamikini to find me and help me use the healing robot, or I may have died.

Maurice then paused and looked down for a moment. He said, "Daniel, I have a confession to make. My final check of the computations of the power required showed we had made a mistake. We have more than enough power for television and radio transmissions such as this, but we needed more power than the single transmission line could provide for the jump."

"Although it increased the risk of our being discovered, I made a linkage with two 10-megavolt electrical transmission lines which run on the other side of the ridges. I did not want to wait any longer, and I knew you were so fired up to go after the coin flips kept picking you to go. As your machine was jumping, one of the reactors failed and the transmission line voltages dipped. The power produced was only 90% of what I calculated we needed. The transferred space from Ontario had a faint burned smell to it. I thought I had killed you. You don't know how relieved I am that you are even alive, much less well. Please forgive me. And tell me, are you still in pain?"

I said, "Of course I forgive you. You had no way of knowing that would happen. As far as the residual pain goes, it feels like general arthritis all over my body, but it is noticeably better every few hours."

Maurice replied, "Glad to hear that! I have already made some adjustments to our equipment and to the transmission line linkages, so future jumps will have more than enough power. Now, how are you and the Kamikini getting along?"

"The Kamikini and I are getting along well, but I have not told them of our plan yet. They are even more compatible with us than we had expected. Later today I will bring two generals into the control room and show them the screen and talk with you again. Perhaps then they will want our help and let us move to their world and out of the terrors of Earth."

As if an afterthought, I mentioned, "Maurice, they also believe in the Creator."

Maurice seemed quite pleased by that revelation. We signed off after agreeing on a time to talk again.

The next communication apparently happened that afternoon with the generals present. I did not know that the generals did not understand what they were seeing. We did not have the expensive equipment needed for three-dimensional broadcasting, so a two-dimensional screen was all we had. The generals were not familiar with such images and did not comprehend them at the time.

Maurice and I were talking about our hopes to help them, using the elementary vocabulary we received from the robot we had sent to their world earlier. Suddenly, Maurice seemed distracted. With the transmitter still on, he stepped aside to deal with some emergency. I heard an audible alarm beeping constantly for several seconds. He came back to the screen looking very scared and anxious.

"Daniel, the government troops have found us! They will kill us for sure when they find out who we are. The extra transmission line taps enabled them to trace our location. Even now they are in the compound!"

My family and his came into the background and got into the sphere. Maurice went on, "We must make the jump immediately, then destroy our equipment by a timer after the jump. Pray for us!"

He went to the sphere, entered it, and shut the door. I recognized the sequence of light indicators near the sphere. The process takes 12 seconds at full power. At eight seconds, troopers entered the control room. Two ran to the door of the sphere and began to beat on it. One went immediately to the console in front of the screen and began to throw switches and push buttons. I was screaming at him from my end.

At 12 seconds the sphere was still there and smoking. It started to glow red then orange to white at 15 seconds. I saw the trooper pry up the cover over the main self-destruct switch for the complex. Not knowing what it was, but thinking it would stop the sphere, he pushed it.

I heard and saw explosions all around the foolish and terrified soldier. The screen went blank and silent, except for my screaming at this end. The idiot had killed them all! The emotional trauma of losing my family and friend, with the physical pain I still felt, and the sudden knowledge I was trapped on a strange world without other humans was suddenly overwhelming. I could hear my struggle with the generals and my locking them in. The recording continued until the Kamikini let the generals out of the room and it was silent.

This time, Maniho and Leahu understood what was on the screen. Each had one arm on my back and one on my upper arm. I looked at them and saw tears. They knew the loss of loved ones. We were brothers in pain.

The loss was still great. I broke down and cried bitterly. I cried out for my loved ones. *Aimee! Maurice! My children!*

After several minutes I felt better and became calmer. Maniho asked gently, "Are you all right this time, Daniel?"

I rubbed my face with a cloth and said, "Yes, I am all right. I am stunned by the death of my family and friends. Seeing it even this time hurts a great deal. Yet it has brought back my memory. I now remember who I am and why I came."

Looking at them both, I spoke softly, "Knowing you makes the aloneness seem less intense. I would like to be alone to grieve for a while. Please let me go to my room."

Maniho says, "May I post a guard by your door? If you should run away again, the Makurani may find you and kill you."

"Certainly."

As we walked to my room, Maniho directed two soldiers to come to stand guard outside the door. Maniho and Leahu asked if I wanted to be called for the evening meal. "No, I think I will need some time to consider the weight of what I have seen. I will need to be alone for a while."

Maniho said, "We will check on you this evening and in the morning. If the guards say you are sleeping, we will not disturb you. We wish you well in overcoming your pain. It seems all creatures of Ahueha such as you and we must face grief the same. May your sleep bring healing."

I thanked them and shut the door. Every Kamiki knows my pain. But each alone bears his own pain. *Tonight, I bear mine alone.* After the door was shut, I placed my hands high on the wall and looked down at the floor. Always the questions. *Why me? Why my family? Why my friend?* I beat on the wall and cried bitter tears. *How could my God leave me like this? Does he not know my hurt, my aloneness, my feelings of abandonment?*

For hours I let myself feel the hurt and the pain. I cried. I yelled. I sat and stood and lay down in numb hurt. A dagger was in my heart, and only tears through time could wash it away. Though it would rust away, the stain of its steel would be on me all my living days. The scar, like all other scars, would shrink with age but never completely disappear.

At such times, it was natural to feel sorry for myself. Rather than fight it, I turned it into prayers of deep pain. Like so many of the psalms, my feelings poured out of my mouth and into the ears of God.

In late evening, when most were asleep, I had poured out all of my pain to God. When my soul was at rest, God reminded me of the pain he bore. As a fellow sufferer, he showed me the greater picture of his works. Though I myself did not fully understand, I knew he understood and was hurting with me. He found no fault with my tears and pain. He comforted my heart with a strange peace I have felt only a few times. In this comfort I found a quiet place for a while. In the depths of my pain I felt he was somehow my friend.

"Lord, I don't like this. I don't understand it. If it be possible, may they somehow live. If not, may you keep them safe with you. And may you comfort me. I feel very alone. I need you to be my peace."

In the late hours of the night I rested a heavy sleep with restless dreams.

I awakened after 12 hours to early afternoon the next day. By the time I get cleaned up and dressed, Maniho and Leahu were waiting outside my door. The guards had informed them of my being up.

"How are you, Daniel?" Asked Maniho softly.

"I still have pain inside, but I am doing better. I feel a little lost. My family was the main reason I came. Now they are gone. I will need some time to assess my situation and move on with my life. My purpose seems to be tied up with your world now. I have no way back to Earth. In the meantime, have you seen any activities among the Makurani?"

"No, we have expected but have not seen any movements."

"Then may I see the sphere I came here in?"

They nodded and led me to a large storage room near my office area. There on the paving stones was a sphere identical to the one in the recording. I recognized it immediately as my sphere. I searched inside while Maniho watched. Leahu requested leave to meditate and attend to other duties. He said the rest of the elders were meeting to discuss important matters.

Inside the sphere I found a few additional items which would help us on this world. There were repair robots, another healing robot, a navigational system, and several electronic aids useless away from Earth.

"Maybe I can convert them to other uses," I told Maniho after describing their functions.

After sitting inside the sphere, I reflected on the many months of planning and preparation which led to my being here. How differently it turned out from our hopes and dreams! I had to adjust to living with those beings away from human contact. They believed in God, so maybe I could learn to live with and enjoy them. Even so, I felt more like Gulliver in the land of the little people.

SECTION II

Who Was I?

Chapter 11: Rise to Fame

Now that the door to my mental house full of memories had unlocked, the door opened up and swung wide open, inviting me to come in for a long leisurely stroll. After the evening meal, I went to my room to revisit the past. There above the bed was a parade which marched through the screen of my mind for several hours.

At first it was a hodgepodge of bits and pieces, some pleasant and some excruciating. I decided to get some control over the chaos by starting with my earliest memories and going year by year. The chronology unfolded more or less as follows.

HUMANITY 2.0

2008-24

I was born in Tampa, Florida. My father, Eric Davidson, was proud to have a first born who was a son. He was a true Christian who converted as a boy just before the year 2000. As a manager over computer systems analysts, he delighted in the logical consistency of the New Testament in accordance with cold-case detective analysis. He named me Daniel which means, "God is my judge." For my middle name, he gave me Wayne which means "burden bearer." Wayne was an old name for wagonmakers, called wainwrights. Often, he told me he had a sense I would be special. Of course, I liked this but always thought he was biased like any good father.

My earliest memories included many times with Mom. She was a rare mother who did not work outside the home, at least until after the last child "left the nest." We often went to the store and shopped together.

She talked to me about whatever we were doing and wanted to help me learn. We laughed a lot. And we hugged a lot.

Sometimes she would cry about something which went wrong. She would tell me why it hurt. I did not want her to cry, but she said it always made the pain better. I learned that tears are our friends and that boys can cry too. But they may have to cry in private.

My Dad included me in many of his home projects. We would build things and go fishing and hunting together. Sometimes Grandpa Mike would go with us. I always felt big with them, and they helped me feel big.

I had no siblings until I was five. By age ten, I had a brother and a sister. When bullies attacked them, I wanted to take care of them. Dad said I should only help when they were being seriously hurt. Otherwise, they would never learn to take care of themselves.

Boy, did I remember picnics and movies and vacations! Birthday parties and visits to relatives! My favorite party was on my sixteenth birthday. We invited the ten prettiest girls I knew. Each kissed me on the cheek. I thought I had reached the top of the mountain.

My other fondest memories of youth were getting awards in high school for high academics, starring in high school sports, and dating a beautiful girl for my three years of high school. I skipped two grades along the way and graduated high school in three years at age 16. I was already a National Merit Finalist and was all-state twice in two sports. When I was in college, I also participated in medieval swordplay and exceled at Kung Fu.

2024-27

I went on an excellent academic scholarship at age 16 to the University of Orlando, which by then had a high achieving, but virtually unknown, department in biomedical engineering. A few professors in other areas were quietly researching nuclear fusion and quintuple sensory telecommunication. There they also had some of the leading researchers for NASA working on how to set up a colony on Mars.

The head of biomedical engineering, Dr. Jose Caliente, a brilliant South American, had already collaborated extensively with computer technicians, psychiatrists, geneticists, and surgeons in developing robots which could operate surgically at a finer level than any human could do.

(The robots I brought to Ontario were the latest miniaturized versions resulting from that work.) The psychiatrists helped his team determine hormone and catalyst implant effectiveness from microsurgery in the brain and internal organs. The most helpful surgeon was a Nobel Prize winner from Egypt.

After that, Caliente's team investigated laser and micro-electromagnetic techniques for operating with an electron microscope. This led to incredible breakthroughs. They were the first researchers to discover how to completely alter the genetic code in DNA molecules by breaking the molecules apart and recombining them as they chose. The most critical technique in the process was discovered by Dr. Caliente as he was doing yard work. He went immediately to the laboratory to try it, and it worked.

Then an incredible thing happened. The United Nations learned of his work and provided heavy funding to him and his team in 2021 for the conception of Superiors, as he called them, in women in Third World countries. They surveyed those countries to enroll volunteer women under age 30. Then they sent teams to go to various locations in those countries to harvest an egg from each woman, impregnate it with the Superior sperm substitute with all dominant genes, then implant it in the woman's uterus to continue the normal womb cycle. The child born was expected to be far superior to other children born of two natural parents. This process began heavily in secret in 2022 in 10 different countries, and 100,000 Superiors were born in 2023. By the time I came under his wings in 2025, there were over 200,000 Superiors alive and thriving in those countries and 15 more.

Seeing my excellent promise early in the second semester of my freshman year, Dr. Caliente took me as his only student assistant. I went into his effort wholeheartedly and put most of my free time into this magnificent work. We were excited fanatics about this process, working long hours six, sometimes seven, days a week. I was first heavily involved in preparing the Superior sperm specimens. Not long after that I was assigned the responsibility of being the first member of the team to follow up on the Superior babies to check their early progress. I quickly discovered that there were still many birth defects in the Superiors, and most turned out to have very average genetic traits based upon size, weight, early psychological tests, and other types of medical measurements. It appeared that the inferior genetics of most of the women were still being passed on to all of the babies. Only a small percentage of the newborns seemed to have the markers we expected.

I pondered this for several days before reporting the findings to Dr. Caliente. I also advised him that we should go to implanting a totally prepared fertilized egg instead of just using a sperm substitute. He agreed wholeheartedly, and we began production immediately. In place of the former method, we then sent teams to place a Perfect zygote (the single celled embryos that were like a fertilized human egg) into each volunteer woman.

It was very time-consuming to produce the zygote cells for implantation into the willing women. Within a few weeks, I found a way to increase the speed in making the zygotes that enabled us to produce over 1,000,000 each year. We also expanded the range of choices of Perfects, as Dr. Caliente now called them, by developing master codes for a dozen new human types, but all in a new light brown master race.

And it was just in time. Other countries had heard of the process, especially creating and birthing the Perfects, and begged to be included. By the time I graduated in 2027 after three years at the university, his sixth year of running the UN project, we had over 2,000,000 babies in 40 countries.

In 2026, he incorporated our work as The Perfects Projects, Inc, with me as an Executive Vice President because of the many ideas that I had contributed to the cause. We continued to use the university as home base, paying them from the vast amounts of funding coming into the corporation.

During those college years, my old feelings that I would someday do some magnificent work to help the world began to resurface. The power in our hands was immense. We could alter human life forever. No more genetic disease. Tendencies to mental illness would disappear in future generations. We could adjust muscularity potential, height, flexibility, intelligence tendencies, and gender. Virtually eliminating aging was now possible. We had the tools to even alter racial codes, or even create new races. We could foresee a master race, growing up in loving homes of humans delighted to see their children become super men and super women. The long-awaited glorification of the human race was here at last after thousands of years! And I was at the epicenter of the miracle.

Although raised in a Christian home in early years, I was slipping away from these basics. Dr. Caliente in that era was a major intellectual proponent of the Darwinian theory of human origins. His influence on me was bigger than life. After our work together had resulted in placing Perfects in so many countries by 2027, he had become a household name around the world. He made sure those who worked on the project with him received their share of credit. Three other professors and I, the only student in the group, shared the recognition along with him as the members of the propagation team. We were almost as highly acclaimed as he was. We also had hundreds of doctors around the world doing the actual implantation and monitoring the babies' development in the womb and after birth.

He took me with him to many press conferences and technical seminars. I became more than a disciple, even though still in college. Now that we could create a super race, the Christian story sounded less important than the realization of the secular humanist ideal of superior humanity. The ideal of those like Caliente had won. Who needed a savior from 2,000 years ago when we now had the promise that with genetics and microsurgical robots you could live forever in a constantly improving world?

My parents were horrified, of course. They said Grandpa Mike (who had passed away) would have been horrified at what our corporation was doing, accusing me of helping to destroy the human life that God had created. They were so against me that I had to avoid seeing them altogether. This further fueled my conviction that I and my colleagues were correct. We were the ones who would lead the world into its greatest era of progress. And we were not alone in this thinking. The super-majority of scientists of the world community agreed with us.

In May 2027, I had graduated with honors and by that time received 12 honorary doctorate degrees from universities in 7 countries. I was also a multi-millionaire, but only this work had my attention. Its magnificence consumed me.

2028-43

Using implanted nanite markers on their hands and foreheads, we followed the growth and developments of all these children. The United Nations started a worldwide banking and bookkeeping system using similar markers on the hands and foreheads of other humans mainly to enable us to track these super humans as they spread across the continents. Many older sub humans, as we called them sometimes, refused to get the markers. We allowed them to continue using credit cards and other external means for the time being. By 2035, however, all countries were marking babies born in hospitals, regardless of race. That is, except for the children of the many religious fanatics, mostly the evangelical Christians.

Those religious fanatics were a constant nuisance. Warning of disaster and ruin, they irritated us every chance they got. We just laughed at them. Our work was going superbly. Who cared what the nuts thought? Besides, the world has always had those who fought great progress. We let them say what they wanted. We were able to create a new world, and they could not stop us.

In 2033, Dr. Caliente had turned the reins of our corporation over to me as the Chief Executive Officer (CEO). Everything was doing well except for the minority of scientists who still opposed our work. Our most distinguished and difficult opponent was a pure researcher and astronomer who at one time was a world class chess player and outspoken Darwinian evolutionist. After he had received Nobel prizes for first biology and later astronomy, he delved into the works of the Intelligent Design proponents, mostly with the aim of pointing out where they had used poor logic or bad science. As a result, he instead came to believe in a creator. Researching the major world religions led him to trust the accuracy of the Bible, especially the New Testament. This led to what he called his "dramatic conversion to Yeshua Ha Mashiach." He preferred to call him by his Hebrew name.

From then on, he saw us as the greatest enemies of God. I took up the gauntlet as his primary debater. Facing each other often in televised debates, we became bitter enemies. He often upstaged me with brilliant arguments and observations, and I hated him the more I saw him. The world press favored the genetic cause and made every effort to discredit him and Intelligent Design. By 2040, world opinion was turning against all who opposed our cause, and especially against all outspoken professing Christians. Soon none of our opponents were able to get any hearing, including that irritating eminent scientist.

By the year 2043, the new race had performed phenomenally. There were over one billion of them all across the world. The oldest were 20 years old and had graduated from universities as world class athletes and honor students. They were winning every conceivable kind of scholastic award as well as setting records in athletic competitions. In the Olympics, the teenagers were setting incredible world records. The young men were averaging 6'4" tall, the young women were around 6' even. Their average IQ under the classical testing systems was 190. In the United States and other countries, the leaders changed laws and constitutions to allow them into public office as early as 12 years of age. The leaders of many countries and much of the United Nations which promoted their development were young men and women of this race as young as 14 years old. Over 50% of all babies being born after 2038 were of this race, and the percentage kept rising dramatically. A new humanity was taking over from the old, tired, genetically declining ones. We were living in the Utopia that so many had only dreamed of.

FAMILY LIFE UNFOLDING

In June 2027, I had married a strikingly beautiful and gentle woman, but she knew my first love was this work. I met her at a party and was intrigued that she did not want to have sex with me like most women. We dated and hit it off on many levels, getting married in a quiet ceremony away from paparazzi a few months later. She delighted in having such an influential and brilliant husband, but she sometimes fussed about my long hours anyway.

We had decided the world was just too crazy back then, and our lifestyles too hectic and stretched, for us to bring children into the world, even from the Perfects. However, she became pregnant in early 2041. We decided to keep the child, and our son was born later that year. He proved to be a tremendous blessing to us. We were very thankful to have such a wonderful thing by accident. To ensure he would not grow up alone, we then tried to have another child, and she was born in late 2043.

Many of our friends and fans could not understand why we did not have children who were from the Perfects. We had discussed it, and we decided that having some of the Perfect children ourselves might be a distraction from all of the other people in the world having Perfects. But of course, our children grew up in a world full of excitement, scrutiny, and paparazzi. They were both highly intelligent and healthy anyway, and we were quite proud of them.

Life on Earth was good, incredibly good indeed. And yours truly had become the most admired and renowned person in all the world.

Chapter 12: Fame to Shame

The Unexpected

It was during the 2030's that our team members across the world began to notice some problems we had not considered. Our computer tracking showed some increasing tendencies among the Perfects borne out by their general behavior. The children of the new race knew almost no pain and suffering as did those in the old races. Perfect health, superior intelligence, and beautiful bodies were their birthright. We had expected that they would be model citizens in their relationships with others. However, we started hearing news stories of situations in which the Perfects did not respond as we had expected.

On some occasions, we heard that regular humans and even Perfects were at times seriously wounded by accidental or intentional situations. In such cases we found that the Perfects did nothing to help the ones who were wounded and hurting, even among their own. There were some cases where it appeared that one or more of the Perfects might have even killed someone else who was screaming in pain unrelenting or showing strong signs of weakness. It seemed the Perfects could not tolerate screaming and certainly not weakness, even among their own. And they were too clever to ever be caught with enough evidence to even charge them with wrongdoing.

By their late teens, those from the new race started seeing the rest of us as burdens. We were sickly and ugly and aging. We required expensive medical attention and psychiatrists and could not always understand what was obvious to them. We were inferior to even the Perfect children of ten years of age. Our decision making and leadership abilities were less than theirs at preteen level. A few persons such as Caliente and I could keep up with them longer, but by the time they were 17, they had passed the best of us.

The Perfects already in positions of power would often promote reducing benefits to the older ones in order to promote their new kind. We had taught them we were now sub human, and they believed it. In our zeal, we had never even considered this happening. Our Perfect children were turning their backs on the ones who created them!

To our amazement, they were totally without compassion!

Most of us on the team, and especially Caliente, continued with the work, saying this was only right and that they had expected it. They said it made sense under the Darwinian concept of survival of the fittest. We often saw that animals in the wild would turn on the weakest of their kind and even kill them. So why should we expect our Perfect creations to be any different?

Privately, I was horrified. I had followed Caliente like he was a demi god. Now he looked like a mindless and foolish fanatic, too consumed by personal hubris, and increasing political power, to turn away from his fame. The full impact of what we had done was dawning on me in dramatic fashion. We had superseded the human race and substituted something else. The new race had over one billion persons on the face of the Earth. There was no turning back. It was over.

Surrounded by Caliente and others like him, I felt trapped. World power had enmeshed us along with members of the new race. I needed time to think privately. How could I get away? Proceeding carefully, I told them I wanted time to let my creative powers consider plans for the coming years. I took 30 days off and went with my wife, Aimee, to see her parents. They kept our two children, while we went to a cabin that we owned in the Tennessee hills. After we had settled in and I felt safe to speak honestly, I shared with her my fears and concerns as we were sitting in front of a fire on a cool day in early March. To my surprise, she broke down and cried.

She said, "O Daniel, I thought I was the only one who felt that way! I have been afraid of you and your colleagues for the last few years. I did not know you also had concerns."

I answered, "I have just recently stepped back mentally to look at the results. I thought we were bringing a long-awaited time of Perfection and peace to the world. Instead, we have created monsters without compassion. I believe it is only a few years until the world will see suffering such as never seen before. This new race is still quite young and yet growing quickly impatient with the old races."

"Daniel, what can you do now? Can you stop it?"

"I do not see how. All I see ahead is horror. It is just like the events my religious fanatic opponent said would happen. He does not look like such a nut at this point."

Aimee took my hand in hers. She said softly, "Honey, I have wanted to ask you this for a long time. With all of this facing us, is there any way we could talk to him?"

I exploded into anger and jumped up shouting, "What?! Are you crazy?! How could I go to a man like that? He has been my arch enemy for years now. You just do not walk up to someone like that and say, 'Hello, arch enemy, may we talk about how I helped destroy the world, just like you said?'"

I had marched away from the fire to the other side of the room and placed my hands on the door frame. She went slowly over to the fire and stood by the pillows where we had made love the night before. She waited for me to calm down a bit and said as she looked down at the fire, "Honey, you need to know something important."

Still flushed, I glanced back at her. "What is it?"

Slowly, she looked at me then looked down at the fire again. "What I am about to share with you may be difficult for you to hear, so I am praying that you will be able to let me tell you about it without going crazy. Can you please do that?"

I waited a bit and then said, "All right, I will give you my full attention and allow you to say what you need to say." I then sat down at the other couch across from her and waited for her to share what she had to say.

She began slowly and soon warmed up to her normal pace. "At the debates I often saw his wife in shops and in restaurants. One time we came face to face. She was friendly and always spoke to me. One afternoon while you and he were preparing for the debate that night, I saw her in the hall of the hotel. She invited me in for a cup of coffee in her room. I went and we had a good talk."

She looked to see if I was getting angry. I was a little, but she went on, "We usually met at each debate after that.... We became friends.... We have written to each other several times since the last debate."

When she paused again, I said quietly, "Okay, go on."

"Well..., I think he is someone you could still talk to. From what she says and from what I have seen of him, he would be kind when you meet him. He won't make you feel uncomfortable."

I felt she was right. Even in the debates, he never attacked me. He only attacked my ideas. It was crazy, but a warmth was settling over me as I thought of him. Finding him and talking to him suddenly changed from a crazy thought to become my one desire, my only hope.

We slept that night, then found the desire to find him was stronger the next day. She made some calls and found he was living in Montana on a ranch. Due to the persecutions, he had moved out of the public spotlight and set up housekeeping in a secluded area. We packed up our belongings at the cabin, loaded up the sky car, and headed to where we heard the ranch was.

We flew on normal skyways until we reached northern Idaho and spent the night there. Then we left the next morning and flew slowly at low altitudes backtracking into Montana. This took almost an entire day before we found the ranch in western central Montana.

Several times the urge to turn back had welled up inside me. Each moment it happened, Aimee and I talked it out. There seemed to be no other real alternative. We kept on going.

Now, as we passed over a ridge the ranch came into view. I felt like I was choosing to enter a dragon's lair, that only death could result from proceeding on. I stopped the car in midair. Looking back now, I see that the turning point of my life was the decision we made at that very moment.

The Turnaround

I flew the car down to near the front door and parked it. We apparently had set off a security system, because by the time we got out of the car the owners were already on the front porch. I took Aimee's hand in mine and we walked up to the porch.

I spoke first, saying, "Dr. Monterre, we meet again. Except this time, I do not come as an enemy, but we both come as a disillusioned couple hoping you can provide us your help."

He replied, "I must say, Dr. Davidson, that you might very well be the last person I ever expected to try to find me, and especially to ask for my help." He looked at me for a moment and seemed satisfied that I was there honestly, and so he offered, "I know it took you a while to get here from wherever you were today. Why don't you both come in and relax for a few minutes. Then we can talk. And in case you need it, the bathroom is down the hall to the left." He smiled broadly and waved us in.

We went in and refreshed ourselves. We met in the family room and began by introducing our wives, Aimee and Michelle. We all agreed to call each other by first names from then on. Our wives shared a big hug and then left the two of us in the family room while they went into the kitchen to talk and to plan the next meal.

Maurice asked me to give details about what had happened to cause me to seek him out like this. I told him how we thought the Perfects were so incredible, but we had realized that we had created narcissistic beings without compassion even for those like themselves. I was genuinely concerned that there would be some kind of worldwide Holocaust in the future when the Perfects used their positions to eliminate the older humans like us and even our natural-born children.

He listened intently and did not seem at all shocked. I was surprised when he lowered his head and whispered some prayers. Then he looked at me and said, "Daniel, this is what I had foreseen years ago. I did not know exactly how it would turn out, but I knew that these new humans you had created and distributed across the globe would prove to be one of the most monstrous things that ever happened to mankind. When we first started our debates, I had just finished reading C. S. Lewis's book, The Abolition of Man, and saw that what you are doing was exactly what he had forecast. Little did any of us ever realize it could turn out as bad as what you have said. This is profoundly serious indeed."

I pleaded, "Do you think there is anything we can do to turn this around? Every way I look at this I see horrible happenings in the next 15 to 30 years."

"No, I don't. We should take some time to pray about this and see what God believes we should do."

I reminded him, "You know that I am not a Christian and that I've opposed all people who believed in a God, especially the God of the Bible. And now I see that I've made something horrible. We have substituted our own idols, our own creations, for the living God, if such a being truly exists."

"Daniel, you know that I have looked at the evidence against Darwinism that loudly and clearly reveals this marvelous universe was intelligently designed. The debunking of spontaneous generation almost 200 years ago, the lack of evidence for the thousands of transitional forms that would have been required in the fossil record, and the incredible complexity within single celled animals all shout out that there is a God. Further, the marvelous DNA molecule in every living cell is an information processor of incredible rank. Then I studied the major religions of the world to see if any of them had a credible description of the attributes of God. I found only the Bible to be a trustworthy historical source for knowing about God. And I believe you also have come to see that this is true."

"Maurice, after all I've been through, I feel so stupid and ignorant and even weak. I studied the Bible many times in my youth and so I know what it says. I know that the resurrection of Jesus Christ is one of the best documented actual events of recorded history. But only now have I been able to once again look to see if I could ever know him as other people like you say they do."

"Daniel, my soon-to-be brother in Christ, let's call our wives back into the room and we will pray for you to become a Christian, even as you may have guessed your wife already is."

We called them back in and Maurice explained what we had been talking about. We spoke for a while about what the Bible said about Yeshua of Nazareth. We talked about his life of teaching and saying that he was the anointed king, the Messiah, of the Jews. He had come to save all mankind from a very real and evil force, which was Satan and the one third of the angelic emissaries who used to live in God's home domain. We talked about Jesus' death on a Roman cross, his burial, his shocking resurrection on the third day, his 40 days of appearing to his disciples, and his being translated back into the home domain of God the father.

Then with Aimee holding my hand, I prayed to God for the first time in years. I told him I believed that he is the God of the Bible, the real and true God, the creator and sustainer of everything. I affirmed that I now accepted Jesus Christ as my Savior, exchanging my awful sinfulness for the beauty and glory of his righteousness and riches in heaven. Then Aimee put her arms around me and we both wept joyfully and loudly for several minutes.

I already knew that immersion in water was the official act of entering into the New Covenant life of Christ. It symbolized that I had died to my old life and was buried in the water and then raised into a new life. After Maurice pronounced over me that I was being immersed into God the father, God the son, and God the Holy Spirit, he said that I would then receive the gift of the Holy Spirit as people have done for 2,000 years.

The next few days we talked about what should be done at this point. I knew I had to publicly denounce everything that I had done and believed in the past. The four of us agreed to pray for God to give us wisdom on how to do that. We also agreed that Aimee and I should go back and bring our children there. The Monterres were wonderfully hospitable in saying that they had more than enough room in a secondary house nearby to allow us all to live there as long as we wished.

Aimee and I went back and then got our two teenage children. I was shocked to find out that they had already prayed with their mother to receive Jesus Christ as their own Lord only a few months before. I realized that I was so blinded by work that I had lost touch with what was going on in my own family. However, I was extremely glad that they had done so. I was already concerned that they might not accept Christ as Lord and that we would be a divided family. Instead, we were now a new family seeking to walk after the God who was, is, and will be.

It would be too difficult to try to pack up all our possessions and take them with us to the Monterre's ranch. Paparazzi and news media were all around our primary residence. However, we put out the word that we were establishing a new vacation residence and would need to transfer many of our possessions to the new location. We placed them in oversized truck containers and had them shipped to the nearest railroad station. We then set up for someone to take them off the train in an unknown location from where they could secretly have them delivered to the Monterre's ranch without anyone else knowing.

We went back to the ranch again in such a way that we were able to keep people from following us. The four of us adults talked at length about the way forward. We even involved our teenage children at times, Tim and Natalie, for their opinions. On the third day there, I received a message on my encrypted communicator saying that I had been asked to speak at the United Nations in about two weeks in New York City. We talked this over and decided to have me use this occasion to denounce my previous passion.

I prepared a short speech because I knew it would not be long into the speech before I would probably be shouted down by the shocked and unbelieving room full of representatives. I wrote the full text out so it could be released over all of the international media outlets, especially the massive international Internet. It read as follows:

(Greetings to those in attendance and other formalities)

To the people of the world, today I offer my sincere thoughts on the current state of humanity. We are in transition, as we have known for some time, from the older races of humanity to a new race of superhumans. Dr. Caliente and I were among those who spearheaded this effort and have made our careers from it. We know that we will go down in history as some of the greatest innovators who impacted humanity at the deepest levels.

While denying the existence of a supernatural God, we pursued the ideals of Darwinistic secular humanism in seeking to evolve mankind to a higher state. And in many ways, we succeeded beyond our dreams. And we witnessed a surprising development. We have discovered that the new race we created is phenomenally narcissistic and devoid of basic human compassion for fellow humans. This drove me to realize that there is a God of the universe, and that he is the God who is revealed in the Bible. It turns out that Jesus Christ truly is our only hope, and I have recognized him as my Savior and the Lord of Creation.

With regard to our new race I do not see how we can turn back the clock. I strongly recommend from this day forward that we do not inseminate any more women from the old race with our Perfect offspring. These offspring may have children of their own, but that should be the only way that these bizarrely self-centered creatures are able to propagate.

I totally regret my hand in all of this, and I ask all of my fellow humans to please forgive me for the foolishness that I have participated in. More than anything, may God have mercy on my soul for what I have done.

Maurice set up the dissemination of the message content to go out over the Internet and all other media sources at the moment I began speaking. We then prepared for me to escape New York by using a route that could not be traced back to where we lived now.

All of the events and planning activities that led up to making the speech are still a little bit of a blur. I packed for the trip, got there by a convoluted route, and set up in the hotel room. I attended the usual special dinners and meals that we shared with the most eminent of the delegates, especially those from the United States and its allies. That led up to my waiting in the ready room behind the main podium, conversing with friends while not revealing the content of my speech. And yes, they were probing constantly.

On the evening of November 11, 2052, I walked up to the podium and took out my brief notes. At that moment I also pressed a button on my communicator that caused the written text to go out to the world electronically. Looking at the expectant audience I began, speaking faster than normal. Shortly after I mentioned Jesus Christ, many rose to their feet and began to yell and wave their arms in anger. I hurriedly finished my speech without pausing and left quickly with the prearranged personal security detail. As we got into the van and drove away, there were many demonstrators already in the street making finger gestures my way and some even chasing after the car. I was done on the world stage. My previous great fame would now become infamy as the majority of the world abruptly turned against me. I could only go back into hiding with the Monterres, hoping no one would find out that my family and I were there.

Chapter 13: The New Path

So now I was in a place where I never ever expected to be. I had no idea what lay ahead. My life had been carefully planned with many goals achieved in the last few decades, and now everything was overturned. I was on a new path that was remarkably unknown to me.

We had prearranged for the security detail to take me by a series of vehicle changes to a particular place in the Midwest. I released them there and took the next leg of my planned route. After a few more changes in direction, I ended up back at the Monterre's ranch and with my family. Aimee and the teens were extremely glad to see me back in one piece, but they also knew that our lives were changed forever. For the next several days, we busied ourselves with making the house we were living in truly a home. It had been built as a cave house that opened on the side of the mountain and extended into the mountain. We were able to use the natural cave-like temperatures to give us a more economical heating and cooling system.

After we settled into our new home at the ranch, Maurice proceeded to update me on the world conditions of the last few years. As with many people who are in positions of great authority and influence, I was very unaware of what was happening across the globe. And, sadly, I had not cared that spiritual conditions in the world had gotten to be so bad by then. He showed me dozens of examples of the Perfects acting contemptuously of the older races. And by 2051 spiritual conditions had become very dark worldwide, even in America.

Biblical Christians were being specially targeted and persecuted severely. Millions of Christians had been killed, and others had lost their careers or had family members taken away from them by force. Many of them were forced into human trafficking. There was mass raping, pillaging, and murder while government agents said and did nothing. When questioned, some of the authorities would say something like, "They brought this on themselves." There were more deaths of Christians due to unlawful persecution in the year 2051 than in any other year of recorded history. And that reign of terror continued unabated to that time in 2052.

On top of all this, the Roman Catholic Church had begun serious and bizarre capitulation to the other forces of the world. They kept quiet about the world situation and insulated themselves, sometimes creating gated communities where they could hide. In several countries they signed ungodly agreements to avoid the severe persecution of their people.

Maurice had foreseen this several years before our arrival. He had been praying about how he should prepare for the future. In a dream he envisioned a camouflaged refuge in a valley between two ridges. This would serve as a hiding place for him, his family, and a few friends if needed. He had it built in a time when there was less persecution and fewer people in the government and other agencies who were spying on people using satellites and drones.

On the other side of one of the ridges he built his test center and experiment station. It was disguised as a type of warehouse distribution center. He arranged to have some shipments that would come in and out, and he kept some semi-trailers outside to add to the illusion that this was a distribution center. In front of the test center was a good two-lane road that could handle the traffic without damaging the pavement. He placed a huge camouflaged roofing structure over the Valley for over a quarter mile that was over 100 feet above the ground at the highest point. This gave him, and later us and a few others, a lot of freedom of movement outside without fear of being discovered by overhead surveillance. He also had an extensive security system placed around the perimeter that he continued to augment over time.

Maurice was very much into healthy eating and good nutrition. He set up a large ranch to the left of the warehouse where he had people raising various kinds of livestock along with some large gardens with a wide variety of vegetables, fruits, and berries. There was a small slaughterhouse that humanely prepared the animals for our use. The ranch supplied most of our needs, and many times we had the freshest available foods to enjoy.

From the income of his previous types of work and investments, Maurice had purchased and maintained a large number of state-of-the-art pieces of construction equipment, some quite huge. They were highly automated using GPS coordinates operating from three-dimensional designs. He purchased supplies elsewhere and had them shipped to the site, with his equipment doing most of the actual construction. This enabled him to keep his human contact as low as possible.

Maurice's experiment station enabled us to further extend our knowledge of our physical world, including how to harness the new knowledge about gravitational forces. By the middle of 2053, he was probably the finest expert in the world on gravity, but we knew that the knowledge he had obtained would be abused by the countries of the world if they had access to it. Therefore, we kept it to ourselves. Actually, I asked Maurice to only tell me what I needed to know, so that people could not get to me for the information he had. Little did I realize that he had uncovered a lot more than I would have suspected.

In order to harness the power needed to conduct the experiments with gravity, Maurice and I set up a dummy corporation that clearly shielded who we were in order to bid on the operation of a nuclear plant just over 30 miles away. The nearby location of the nuclear plant was one of the reasons why he set up his operation where he did. We won the bid in late 2053 and set up our most trusted friends to be the high-level managers of the plant. But even the people who worked for us did not know where we lived. We were able to use another company with people very committed to Maurice who were able to place the world's largest extra high voltage cables underground from the nuclear plant to our experiment station. The power that we drew at times from the nuclear plant was large, but not enough to set off any alarms at government agencies who monitored the plant.

And so, we began experimentally researching his new knowledge about gravity waves and frequencies. We were experimenting one day in the summer of 2054 with gravitational phase shifting using a small sphere as the focal point. The sphere was one meter in diameter, and we had an extremely powerful electromagnetic system arranged in a spherical array around it. At first, we could not get it to do what we expected. But Maurice was obsessed with trying to make it work. Sometimes he would go back to the lab when I was home with my family to try new things. One night right after supper he called me on the phone.

He sounded incredibly excited. "Daniel! You have to come to the lab right now. I found something really incredible."

"Well, is it something you can tell me about now? You know how I like to be prepared whenever I show up at a meeting, especially with you, because you are always full of surprises," I said jokingly.

"No, this is way too important. I was totally surprised when I saw it myself, and I want you to experience it like I did."

I hurried over to the lab through the tunnel and went to the laboratory where we were running the experiments. When I got there Maurice could hardly contain himself. He was the most excited I have ever seen him.

I shouted on the way in, "Okay, I'm here. So, what is this great incredible thing that you want to show me?"

"Come over here so I can demonstrate it to you." He already had the system energized and operating. He adjusted a few settings and told me to watch the sphere. When he hit the main activation button, the sphere disappeared.

"Okay," I said, "So you got the sphere to disappear. Where did it go? And can you bring it back?"

He waited a couple of minutes, made a few adjustments to the settings, hit the button again, and the sphere reappeared. Then he went to the sphere and opened it up, showing me some sensing devices that he had placed in it, including a camera that looked through one of the viewing ports. He took the memory card out and took it over to his laptop. Then he started the video, and I watched in amazement as it panned around, showing a landscape with trees and rocks. And they were noticeably different in some ways from what we have on Earth. It also scanned upward and looked at the sky. In the sky above were two twin suns that gave daylight to the landscape.

I stood in stunned silence taking this in. Then I asked him, "What in the world are we looking at?"

Maurice slowly offered, "Honestly, Daniel, I don't know. But I think you and I together need to get more data in order to find out what this means."

After sending the sphere back and forth several times from that place to our own over the next few weeks we made the surprising discovery that we had somehow found a parallel world to our own. And there were no clues in the camera shots of the night sky as to where this was in the Universe. We found we could use the small sphere to transpose space from that world with space from our world. We even tested the air that came back from the other world and found that the chemical composition was a little different from Earth's. The ratios of nitrogen, oxygen, and carbon dioxide were similar to Earth, but the percentages were notably different.

We found that the sphere always returned to the same place on the ground in the other world. Only God could have made something like this so synchronized. But why was he letting us know about it now? And what did he want us to do with the knowledge we had gained?

We decided to discuss this with her family members, because this was much too incredible to keep to ourselves. We spent about three weeks in prayer and fasting to discern what God was trying to tell us and have us do with this knowledge. We knew that whatever God was doing that it would impact our future lives and maybe even the rest of the world.

When we felt peace about continuing to research the other world, we then began sending small drones inside the sphere that could be released and travel on prerecorded routes to gather information using the sensing devices we placed in them. We were shocked to learn that not only were there plants and trees, but also rivers and mountains. More surprisingly still, we found that there were animals that inhabited that world. They had some similarities to animals on our world, but they obviously were distinctly different from the species on Earth. We even had the drones gather hair, urine samples, and fecal samples to test the biological properties of the animals and plants, as well as to determine if they had a DNA structure. They did have DNA, and the structure was remarkably similar to that on Earth. We were also able to bring back some samples of the plants, as well as some recently deceased animals. Making sure we did not have any microbial contamination, we examined these samples carefully. Our discoveries continued to get more amazing as we went along.

As another stroke of "pure good fortune," we also found that by adjusting the settings of our equipment that we were able to send and receive radio wave signals through the interface between the two worlds. That enabled us to communicate in real time with drones and other devices on the other world. It takes almost two seconds to send a message between the Earth and the Moon, and here we had almost instantaneous communication with this other world.

During the next few months, we sent many drones to expand the territory that we had researched. One day in late 2054 we discovered the two inhabited cities of humanlike creatures living there. This completely floored us. We again stopped our research and went into another season of prayer with fasting. This was so overwhelming! After another couple of weeks, we felt God was leading us to go back and learn more about the "people" there.

We focused our attention on discovering more about their situations, their language, and the planet on which they lived. By early 2055, we were surprised to feel that God was leading us to take our families to this other world! We would offer our services to the Kamikini in exchange for us taking refuge there to depart the incredibly growing persecution of Christians on Earth. We felt that our opponents were widening their net and straining to find us. It was only a matter of time, and a fleeting time at that, before they would find where we were hiding out. And we were sure that they would try to kill us and our families and friends. And the rest of the world would celebrate.

By the summer of 2055 we had developed a much larger sphere for transposing space that would enable five of us to travel at one time. It also had plenty of room for supplies and weapons.

During the time we were creating the larger sphere, Maurice had developed the gravity flyer secretly, not even sharing any knowledge of it with me. He had found a way to use atomic fusion on an exceedingly small scale that generated enormous amounts of power that would be needed for the gravity flyer. He obviously kept this to himself so that he could surprise me with a gift when I arrived in Ontario. And he certainly did not want the people in our increasingly darkening world to be able to use the compact fusion generator. We could only imagine the horrible oppression they could instigate with such power.

I made the jump to Ontario six times to transfer supplies and weapons there. Then on my seventh trip I carefully exposed myself to the

Kamikini in order to develop a preliminary relationship with them. This worked out well, and things were going smoothly after several days when the event happened that caused the amnesia that forced me to run away and hide.

SECTION III

Finishing the Job

Chapter 14: The Word and the Sword

After the parade of images and memories played out, I was exhausted emotionally. It was late at night, so I fell asleep easily. Fortunately, no parade of dreams was in my consciousness the next morning, and when I awoke, I felt like a different person. All my past achievements, and even my friends and family, were gone forever. I would grieve their loss for a while, and yet they became irrelevant factors in my present situation. They made me what I was before, but suddenly I was without them and had become someone else. It was as if I went to sleep on one side of a doorless wall and awoke on the other side.

No fear or strong feelings haunted me. A strong but surprising peace gripped my whole being. As I prayed before and after dressing, I sensed a rightness about it all. Proceeding to the breakfast room, I seemed to almost flow in my movements.

At breakfast we were all quieter than normal. Afterward, I asked, "Maniho, please show me the writings which speak of Hakani."

Satisfaction showed on his face. Without a word except for a respectful nod, he led me to a special room inside his residence which looked like a place of worship. Unlike Earth churches, it was bright and cheery. It reminded me of the Crystal Cathedral in California, which was strong enough to withstand the massive Earthquake of 2030, only much smaller with less structure showing. It was a large room, roughly 35 feet square, intended for the two generals, their house attendants, and several guests. The view was of gardens on three sides and the sky overhead. The windows were open slightly, enough to hear birds carry on their constant symphony of joy. In the middle of the room was a collection of writings. The room was set up so that all the activities focused on the center. The furnishings were simple.

Maniho said, "We have often had precious times worshipping Ahueha in this room. It once contained our most valuable furniture and possessions. We hid the sacred writings from the Makurani, who stripped it of its beauty when we could not oppose them, but our personal relationships with Ahueha they could not remove."

He continued as he led me to the table in the middle, "Here are recordings of the words given to us in the last millennium by glorified visitors. They are exact copies that I had my assistants bring out of hiding for you to examine. As one of the leaders, I wrote our memory of the last two visits in the back. Here they are. Please look at them and examine them as you wish."

I wanted to start at the front and read about their whole history. However, my pressing concern was to read the sections on Hakani. The first visitation read as he had said earlier. As I read the record of the second visitation, I asked him about some stains on the page. He looked away and said, "Those are my tears."

I stopped to feel with my new friend. With a sigh, I read on to the end. It read like some of the Old Testament historical books. No flash or flair. No four Gospels. Just the plain facts. In straightforward approach the stories were as he had said, but with more detail.

My electronic wallet had many special functions for scientific use, including one to tell the age of writings. I asked Maniho to give me a writing instrument such as he used to write down these records. He opened a panel under the book stand and pulled out the tool he had been using. He said it had the same kind of ink as used in the book and handed it to me.

I scanned it with the wallet and then scanned the book's last two sections. The wallet analyzed the writing and determined dates for the sections. It predicted dates plus or minus two months for the first section and plus or minus one month for the second section. The wallet's dates fell within a few days of the dates Maniho had written in them.

Again, I checked the second date. The wallet said it was my birthday on Earth. I noticed Maniho was looking at it while standing next to me.

I turned and looked at Maniho, and he looked directly at me. Neither of us said a word, but he knew I must have been taking the prophetic words to heart. And I was. His eyes looked so hopeful and imploringly at mine that I had to look away.

He also looked away, breathing heavily. He went back to one of the knee chairs and began to silently speak to Ahueha. Feeling a kinship with all of his kind, I scanned the earlier portions of the book. Feeling like a Christian reading of the Jews who went before, I read of these whose lives were now enmeshed with mine. The stories of the past glories, the battles with the fallen ones, and the joy and pain of the prophecies unfolded as a play in front of me. My heart was full of awe and reverence for Ahueha.

When an aide came later to the door, Maniho and I both were in silent meditation. The aide motioned to Maniho, and he said to me, "Daniel, the midday meal is nearly ready. Will you come with me to eat?"

Without a word I moved to leave the room and he led the way to the dining hall. His servants had prepared a bountiful meal in my honor. Maniho and Leahu seated me in the place always reserved for their special guest. I felt so overwhelmed I said not a word but ate lightly in silence, nodding and smiling occasionally at different ones who stared at me.

After the meal, Maniho asked me to attend a ceremony the elders had prepared to welcome and honor me formally. I asked to freshen up a bit and join him at his front door. We proceeded from there out of the residence through empty streets to the center square, where all the residents were gathered.

Maniho led me up onto a platform about one yard high. Maniho, Leahu, and I sat on a bench in the center of the stage. After the blowing of trumpets and preliminary prayers and invocations by a few others, Leahu arose and went to center stage to speak.

"Fellow Kamikini, we have waited over forty years for the promise of Hakani. We saw our children and wives killed by the Makurani before our eyes. We implored Ahueha to set everything right. Through an Anakela, he said he would avenge us on the Makurani and lead us into an end time of peace, all by the hands of one from another world. Maniho and I believe that time is now here."

"We have all seen the actions of Daniel as he has defended himself from the Makurani. He is a mighty warrior with superior tools of power and vengeance, a creature who knows Ahueha and came from another world. His own tools have shown him he was born on the date that Hakani was to be born. So far, he has tested the Makurani in self-defense and has killed over 200 of them. Now, we would grant to him our sacred right. None of us can claim it, so the sacred right has been withheld until now. The elders have met, and all agree in desiring to bestow upon him the recognition as our avenger. Bring forth the sword and shield."

Two assistants brought forth a beautiful sword and sheath and a shield of colors to match. The sheath had silver and chromium ceramic with rubies, emeralds, sapphires, and diamonds embedded into it. On the shield was a design showing a Kamikini warrior with uplifted sword from which shined shafts of light, all as a mosaic in the same gems.

Leahu sat down and Maniho went forward. An assistant handed him the sword and sheath. While the other aide held the shield, he pulled the long sword from its sheath. The beautiful white of the ceramic blade sparkled as if flakes of light shone out from within it.

Raising it high in both hands, he blessed it, saying, "Now, O Ahueha, avenge our loved ones as you promised. Bless the bearer of this sword to strike justly in your sight. Protect him with your shield and give him strength to perform your desire with this sword. Bless his every thought and act. May he destroy your enemies completely. May we celebrate his victory."

He then placed it waist high in both hands in front of him, turned to me and said, "Daniel, as you have heard, we desire to give you our sacred right which we ourselves cannot exercise. You alone on our world can take this sword and shield. Please take this for us to act on our behalf. Then your every action against the Makurani will be just. No longer do you need to wait for them to attack you, acting only in self-defense. The right of initiative is yours from now on."

When I hesitated, he waited, then implored gently, "Daniel, we beg you. You alone can do this. None of us can lift a finger in our behalf, but you can do it for us. We have waited so long for Ahueha to avenge us and our families."

I looked around at all the silent and anxious faces. Slowly I rose. I considered turning this down. Somehow, I could not. I walked to Maniho and looked into his eyes. Leahu had come to stand next to him and looked solemnly at me.

Reaching out slowly with both hands palm up, I took the sword. The entire crowd bowed, including Maniho and Leahu. Overcame, I fell to my knees as well. In English I whispered, "May God be with me."

In whispers of their own, they spoke almost in unison, "May Ahueha be with our Avenger."

We were all in silent prayer for some time. I spoke to my Lord as one overwhelmed with responsibility and trust. When a measure of courage and peace came to me, I arose. As I did, they all also arose. Leahu motioned to the trumpeters.

The trumpeters sounded the final processional, and Maniho and Leahu placed me between them and escorted me silently back to the residence. One held the sword in its sheath, and the other held the shield. Back at my room, they asked if they could remove the Makurani sword and shield I had kept until then.

My request was, "Please bury them outside the city. The soldier who carried it tried to take my life, but instead he gave me my life. He was the first being with knowledge of Ahueha who fell at my hand."

They agreed, and Leahu handed the weapons to two aides to do as I asked. He left with them, and Maniho asked, "Hakani, what will you do now?"

"For my name, please continue to call me Daniel. As for what I will do, I must have time to pray and think. It is obvious at this point that I am set up to be your Hakani, but nothing of this has been revealed personally to me. Will you be available if I desire your company?"

"I am available always for you, as are all Kohilo citizens. We will help in any way we may."

"Thank you. These events were emotional, and I need time to deal with them. During this time, I will be reviewing my past to consider this critical point in my life. Afterward, you can help me by telling about the Makurani and the city of Hekanalo. Then I will be praying for wisdom. Please have the Kamikini pray for me, and please let me know of any strange actions by the Makurani."

"Since you left the camp so suddenly, every Kamikini has prayed for you. Some have committed to pray on your behalf several hours per day. Some pray during the night, so prayers go up in your behalf at all hours. We believe our lives are in your hands. We have placed your life in our prayers."

"As for the Makurani," he continued, "We have seen no activity. If they did not know by now that you are back here, then our trumpet blasts will have alerted them. Be prepared for serious and purposeful movements from them without delay."

I looked at him seriously and shared, "This right to be your Avenger is an awesome and heavy responsibility."

"Yes, we know. Remember, our faith is in Ahueha. He is the one we Kamikini look to for protection. Your life and ours are in his care. We trust the same Creator you trust, although we do not always understand his ways. We honor you, but our trust is not in you. Ahueha is the one who provides the victory over our enemies, and they are now yours also."

"Thank you for this insight, Maniho. May you sleep well. Bid Leahu the same."

"Daniel, the same for you. I hope to sleep well, but Leahu will not. He leads the night prayers. That is why you see him so seldom in the daytime."

Impulsively, I reached out and hugged Maniho as I would do it on Earth. He hugged me back. Without looking at his eyes, I entered the room and shut the door.

Lying on my bed for some time, I looked at the sword and shield of the Avenger of the Kamikini. My new role as anointed killer weighed heavily upon me. I reckoned that I was indeed the one chosen to fulfill their prophecies. It was one thing to be given a right as the Avenger, but only full success in avenging them on every Makurani would prove the prophecies to be true.

The bed tossed like the ocean beneath my body, in rhythm with the circus in my head. Hours later, rest came.

Chapter 15: A Fork in the Road

The next day, it was soon obvious whenever I walked around the city that the people treated me with considerable respect. I felt more like a dangerous dog who must be watched closely than like an honored guest. On the one hand, I was favored as the promised Hakani who would soon avenge them. On the other hand, I felt a discomfort from them. They also knew that as Hakani many would die at my hands. A hangman receives much respect.

My every wish they granted, almost before it was uttered. Whatever food I wanted they prepared. I could go anywhere at any time. The people went to any length possible to be sure I felt satisfied. It was humorous at times. Sometimes I felt ashamed. I always felt watched.

Walks in the city were refreshing at first. The shops and businesses along the streets were interesting. I stopped occasionally to speak to a shop owner and asked about his type of business. He was always happy to explain whatever I wanted to know.

The town layout was remarkably simple compared to Earth cities. The main streets spread out like the spokes of a wheel toward the city walls. Cross streets were arranged in circles around the square and were parallel to each other.

The technology and weaponry were like that of seventeenth century Europe. A huge stockpile of spare parts from the time when they had many cities enabled a skilled technician to repair sophisticated equipment. He did it by replacing parts without understanding how they worked. Surprisingly, the ones I talked to did not worry about the why. Each only wanted to make the broken equipment work again.

Several artisans continued to fashion shields and swords and other compatible weapons. I decided that they had come to view it more as art than as a necessity. One told me about the Avenger's equipment. They were made by a skilled, and most respected, weapon maker of over 200 years ago. No one else had her skill or creativity.

Money was not used. A system of trading handled everything. Since each was basically honest and without greed, there were few disputes about comparable worth. Since I was a guest and also a public official, anything I wanted was provided without payment in return.

At my request, some Kamikini took me to their source of water. They would not let us go out of the city until I let a guard go to my room and bring back the sword and shield to carry for protection. He also got my pistol and some grenades, and I always carried my protective suit. After they first sent out scouts to be sure no Makurani were waiting to ambush me, they took me to the waterfall on the main river feeding the area. The equipment for harnessing mechanical power was compact and effective, and they had already installed spare units from other cities in case of failures. The design of it was much more sophisticated than the rest of the daily activities would suggest. Perhaps Maniho would explain it to me later.

Another feature which struck me was that they had no beasts of burden. Outside of a few birds and small animals which stay in and near the city, the Kamikini do not have pets.

The Kamikini left it completely up to me as to when I would begin to fulfill the role they assigned me. Having taken time to remember the past, which was traumatically erased for a while, I was embracing the role of Hakani.

Some scouts reported seeing Makurani approaching the city from the direction of Hekanalo. We hastily returned to the city. Yet it seemed like a useless effort when I realized the Kamikini leave the huge doors to the city open.

Grabbing him by the arm, I stopped one of them as he was walking past me and shouted, "Shut the doors!"

He looked at me and said, "But we never shut the doors. Our generals have ordered this most strongly."

I just stared at him as I considered this. Then I asked, "Why would they order such a thing so foolish?"

He answered back, "We understood the Makurani said they would kill a Kamiki every time any set of the huge city doors was shut. Therefore, the generals told us to leave them open. It would have been a serious mistake to shut them."

I replied, "Then I, your Avenger, would shut them. Show me how."

He took me to the side of the left door and explained how to operate the large rope drive. As I turned the crank, it pulled both doors from against the side walls to a closed position in the middle. The doors overlapped in the middle so that no light showed through the vertical crack. I continued to turn the handle, and the large cross bar lowered from above and rested in the holders. For the first time in over 40 years, the main entrance to Kohilo was closed.

Visibly moved, he then escorted me promptly to the other set of doors at the opposite end of the city. We said not a word to each other. I closed them as well. He seemed both scared and overjoyed at the same time. All he could say to me was, "Thank you, Avenger."

I then requested, "Please take me to Maniho."

He bowed without a word and led me there. When we arrived in Maniho's study, I noticed how like an Englishman's it was. His study was spacious and masculine by Earth standards. The furniture they make of wood that was medium brown in color, somewhat like maple. He had sculptures and paintings of nature scenes on the walls and tables with books and personal items on them. The ceiling had a clear skylight through which one could see the stars at night and suns by day. There were knee chairs and an area where a couple of stuffed couches enabled easy conversation.

Maniho motioned for me to sit near him on a couch. He remained in his knee chair. "Maniho, much puzzles me. I hope you can enlighten me."

With a friendly smile, he said, "Certainly. How can I help you?"

"There are confusing differences in your levels of technology. Some machines and devices are rather advanced and others primitive in comparison. Why is this?"

He answered, "Before the Makurani fell from Ahueha's realm, the Kamikini were very advanced. After the fall, Ahueha restricted the abilities of both groups in certain areas such as warfare, in order that the Kamikini would not be totally destroyed by the older and more malevolent Makurani. Now, our abilities in highly technological areas are confined to maintaining what was already here."

We then spent a long time discussing the differences between mankind and them regarding free will and science. He was surprised that Ahueha gives us such accelerated rates of access to greater knowledge. The free will the Creator gives to humans was almost beyond his ability to grasp.

When I asked about the absence of beasts of burden, he said, "The native creatures of this world are either too small or ill-suited for such work. The creature you saw that morning a while back was big but very frail for carrying extra weight."

"Maniho, what can you tell me of Hekalano?"

"Hekalano is a fortified city almost exactly like Kohilo. The walls are the same height and thickness. There are now 3,678 inhabitants there since their attacks upon you. All the remaining Makurani live there. This has been their custom because of the tight grip their leader, General Anakuia, has on them. You would find houses like ours with a central square, since it was once one of our cities. Our world once had dozens of cities like these. The Makurani always lived close to us and warred with us. Now they live in one last city and we live in our last. The end is near, Hakani."

Angrily, I arose and fairly shouted at him, "Maniho, I told you to call me Daniel! You and your people call me Hakani, but I still hesitate to believe I am the mass killer spoken of in your prophecies! This is very solemn and dreadful to me. I have your right of vengeance, but only time will tell whether I am this 'Hakani' for which you have longed."

I regained my composure and sat down heavily. I was surprised by my strong feltings coming out this way. Yet it showed that this whole Avenger and Hakani situation was overwhelming to me. Maniho was not surprised at my emotional strain and looked away, waiting serenely for me to ask more. He knew more than anyone else that this duty was not my personal choosing. And he also knew they needed me to perform the duty.

I regained my composure and said more softly, "I apologize for my outburst. You have been most kind and patient with me. Now then, are there other weapons besides what I have seen so far?"

"Daniel," He paused to let me see he was honoring my request, then he continued, "The personal weapons are as you have seen. They also have weapons for attacking cities such as large crossbows firing 15-foot shafts. Fireballs and boulders attached to the shafts can fly from them over the walls into cities. No weapons such as yours are in their hands. Nevertheless, many are fierce warriors. Without your special weapons, you would have tremendous difficulty against them."

"If I attack them, how will they respond?"

"I believe they would defend themselves courageously as best they can. Because of General Anakuia, you would never be able to rest. He would send the last soldier to death to defeat you. He knows you could be Hakani. And he certainly knows by now that we have made you our Avenger. It will be most difficult to avenge us quickly."

I paused to consider this, then I asked, "Maniho, there are some things I would like to ask Leahu about. May we talk to him now?"

"Yes, he should be awake by now."

As we proceeded to his living quarters, we talked more about the Makurani's usual military tactics. They were skilled and could be cruel. No advantage, however wicked or ruthless, was beyond their pattern. Only the restraints of Ahueha held them back in the past. That was why so few Kamikini remained before the visitation fifty years ago. The Kamikini would not resort to such evil methods.

Leahu was just finishing dressing when we arrived. He smiled and motioned us on in, and we all sat on knee chairs in a circle. Maniho said, "Leahu, Daniel has some questions for you."

Leahu nodded at me, then I started off with some of the same questions I asked of Maniho earlier to get his own version of the events. After a few, I asked the main one I came to him for. "Leahu, I hear you are the closest to being glorified. Tell me of your relationship with Ahueha. What is it like?"

He answered with joy, almost as a child, "It grows into the richest feelings of happiness and fulfillment more each day. As a younger person, I only vaguely sensed his presence. Now, it is as if a veil or cloud is slowly dissipating. He has become more real. His inner speaking to me is increasingly distinct. I come to him as a friend and lover longing to be with the one I love. This is so strong that little else is important. That is why Maniho now handles the daily leadership duties."

"Has Ahueha told you any more about me?"

"Daniel, you would find he cherishes his personal relationship with each of us, even though it is somewhat veiled to you. He tells me little about you, though I ask often to be reassured about you and Hakani. He has chosen to let you and us discover the truth as it unfolds."

He continued, "He has just now as we talk advised me that I can tell you two things, since your asking about these things is a seeking for him."

"First, he advised me to tell you not to fear your anger. It is a tool you need for what lies ahead. When channeled in proper and legal ways, it serves a great purpose. Yet do not let it consume you or cause you to lose touch with him."

"Second, he does not want to use me or others to speak to you again for him. If he does have us do so, it will mean you will have strayed greatly from his voice and must be saved from actions which would harm you or wrong others. If you seek him, then he said he would speak either directly to you or by actions of providence."

I replied, "Thank you, Leahu. Such words were very comforting. And now, may you and Maniho please excuse me to be alone for a while. I need to think and pray."

I went back to my room and cleaned up. Later, as I walked around the palace, I had a strong, intuitive sense that something was very wrong. A heavy, ominous feeling enveloped me. Fear and excitement gripped me at once.

I ran to my room to calm down and found I wanted to do exercises and swing the Sword of the Avenger around. I was jumpy and wanted to use my many weapons. I had an "itchy trigger finger." Anger from nowhere had laid its hand on my mind and heart.

After a short while I tried to shake it off, but it became stronger. By late evening, the feelings were intense. The door to my room was wide open, and two soldiers came rushing up with a message from General Maniho.

They told me his message was, "Please put on your special armor and come with the Sword of the Avenger and His Shield to my study. The Makurani have sent two messengers and they wish to see you."

I did as they said, also packing a pistol with a full magazine. The general met me and said that the messengers claimed they want to see the two generals and me at the front gate. We walked quickly and met General Leahu on the way to the gate.

Maniho whispers, "The Makurani insist on seeing us just outside the gate. This must be a surprise attack. Be careful."

Before we stepped outside the gate, I asked the generals to stand behind me and fall down if any battle broke out. When we went out, the two messengers came forward to speak to us.

One said, "We have heard you are the Avenger, and maybe the Hakani, of the Kamikini. Now we see by your equipment that you have truly been appointed as their Avenger. We bring you a greeting from our General Anakuia."

With that they gave a hand signal, and six soldiers in red and gold stood up and fired their crossbows at me. As the generals ducked, I felt each arrow bounce off my armor. One ricocheted and struck the second messenger in the thigh. In six shots I dispatched the six archers. The second messenger lay at our feet dying of the arrow poison. The other stood in shock.

I shouted at him in controlled anger, "Tell your general that I will not tolerate such attacks! If he wants to meet me with all his troops in one fight to the finish, I will be glad to do so."

The messenger regained his composure and smiled. "We had hoped this would catch you by surprise. Since it did not work, we will go to the next step. You may be able to fight and defeat many troops if the price is not too high for you."

He let this last thought sink in, then he continued, "We found a sphere 10 miles northeast of Hekalano. In it were six creatures like yourself. They were near death, but we brought them back to our city. They were not doing well, but the one named Monterre has spoken in our language and asked about a Daniel. Our spies have found out you are this Daniel. You are not an immortal rescuer as we expected the promised Hakani would be. You are just a creature from another world with tricks and gimmicks."

He laughed in a snarling way and continued, "Nevertheless, we will make sure. Our general offers this trade. We have surrounded this city with 2,500 soldiers. At dawn, we will attack Kohilo to destroy every Kamiki in it. Then the prophecies of the Hakani would not matter. There would be no one to avenge!"

At this, he laughed long and hard. He thought their joke was the height of irony. Then he said, "If you will not defend the Kamikini, we will let you have your own people. We will gladly allow you to come and retrieve them after the battle. If you kill any of our soldiers in defense of the Kamikini, we will tie them up in the public square of Hekanalo and execute them. The choice is yours: your family whom you love, or these Kamikini who mean nothing to you. Either way, we attack at dawn."

He turned and walked away into the forest. As he left the clearing, a trumpet sounded in the woods, and 2,500 voices surrounding the city give a long blood-curdling shout.

I looked at the generals. They had faraway and concerned looks in their eyes. My eyes meet theirs, and we looked at each other for some time.

When I looked away, Leahu spoke quietly, "Maniho and I shall be with all Kamikini in prayer all night. May Ahueha give you superior wisdom and victory."

They escorted me back inside. Each hugged me Kamiki style by grabbing both shoulders and looking into my eyes, this time solemnly. Then they went immediately to the center square to summon all to prayer.

As I walked back to my room, trumpets filled the air with a special call. Many Kamikini passed me as they hurried to prayer. When I got to my room, I wanted to take a short nap, but I could not. I knew I needed a calm inner self, so I spent time in prayer for wisdom, blending my prayers with those of every Kamiki. Then I lay on the bed and meditated for some time, waiting for the decision which must come before dawn.

Chapter 16: Ride Like the Wind

Suddenly, I hit on a plan! I would go to Hekanalo a while after dark and storm the place to find and rescue my loved ones. Then I would take them out in the sphere using the lifter. It should have enough power to lift them out of there and take them to a safe place, maybe one of my shelters. Then I would come to defend Kohilo using my laser weapons. It just might work! I smashed my fist into my hand. It simply must work.

I decided to tell no one here - even my usual attendants who were assigned to warn me of Makurani movements. I knew their schedule, so I picked the first time when they would not be close by to make my move.

By the time darkness settled fully in, I had laid out in my mind a complete plan. I also had the drones make a quiet mid-level search for probable confinement rooms and buildings in Hekanalo. This narrowed down the places where I would look first.

I would go into action after two hours of darkness. I wanted to rest for the two hours and focus on leaving here unseen, but my whole body and soul became restless. A strong urge to put on the plastic armor was surging up within, even though I had no rational reason to do it then. Trusting this urge, I hurriedly put the armor on.

As the last pieces went into place, the normally quiet hallway outside my room erupted into a frenzy of loud voices and the sound of rushing shoes on the stones. I grabbed the nearest weapon, which was the sword, just as the door slammed open. A large figure stood in the dim light with drawn sword, standing in the doorway with another behind.

A loud voice said, "Die, alien!" Then he stepped forward and swung his weapon in an arch designed to cut me in half. I deflected the blow with my sword, matching his strength and stopping the blade. I then thrust my blade forward and into his midsection. He fell at my feet as the other one saw what happened. He yelled and came crashing in. I had just enough time to grab the shield from against the wall before his sword swung down at me. Deflecting the blow as I raised the shield, I followed through with a swing at his head. He ducked and jabbed at my midsection after I overswung to the left. I shifted my hips back, and his jab missed between my shield and torso.

I swung the sword with a backhand motion which backed him away to my left. With that opening, I reached over toward the pistol, but he swung again before I could get it, bouncing his sword off my shield. We traded a few more blows to shields while my mind raced to consider options. Remembering my urge right before they appeared, I purposely exposed myself a little where he could get a blow in under my shield. He thrust his weapon through the opening in my defenses and plunged hard. I was unhurt because of the armor, although I felt it somewhat and stumbled backwards to where I leaned against the wall. With the shield over the "wound", I slid down. My sword was angled up by placing my hand on the floor and resting the hilt on my right thigh.

He relaxed and came over to me. Standing over me, he laughed heartily and lifted his sword slowly to remove my head as a trophy to show everyone his victory. At the point where his sword was pulled nearly all the way back, I lunged up with my sword and thrust it deep into his abdomen, twisted it, and then pulled it out. He stood for a moment stunned and watched as I stood up before him. He saw my stern face fully from the hall lights shining through the door as his life slipped from his body and he fell backward onto the bed.

After gazing for a few seconds at the fallen form, I then heard more commotion from down the hallway. I grabbed the sword with the shield and then ran over and got the pistol and a spare box of shells. Sprinting out the door, I looked in both directions and headed off to the right. At the end of the hall, I turned to the sounds at my left.

More Makurani soldiers were coming this way. Residence servants who would not protect themselves were protecting me by throwing their bodies into the path of the soldiers. This wasted their time as they had to push the Kamikini aside or hack their way through.

So that no more would try to sacrifice themselves for me, I yelled out, "Get out of the way! These Makurani must now face me!" The Kamikini immediately cleared out and left me easy shots at these soldiers. Six shots left no one standing.

I asked one of the servants, "Quick, are there anymore?"

"We heard noises at the front of the residence and saw two go toward your room. When these came, we tried to slow them down. I do not know if there are any others. Should we check for you?"

"No!" I answered. "Let me check. I will not be harmed. But tell me, are Maniho and Leahu all right."

"We do not know. We had no time to see. They told us you were the only important one now."

With that, I took off for their chambers. They were already up and coming to see about me. As we met in the center atrium, we were all are relieved to see each other.

I spoke first, "Oh, I am glad to see you are all right. I feared they may have hurt you to find me."

Maniho replied quickly, "No, my friend, we are fine. They were not concerned about us. They only wanted to find you, and they knew where you would be in this residence. They must have sent someone in earlier to scout out where you stay. We are nothing to them at this point."

"Tonight, perhaps," I answered. "But tomorrow, they will certainly be concerned about you."

He paused, then replied, "True, but this was a surprise strictly for you. We had posted guards to warn us if some came in like this. Were they able to warn you?"

"Two soldiers broke through quickly, but I heard the noises in the hall. The rest were delayed by your servants. Let us go now and see if any are only hurt and need help."

Maniho and I rushed back and found six servants were dead, while two were bleeding from their sword wounds. I got the healing robot and used it to surgically sew up the cuts and administer scar-reducing chemicals which fit their body chemistry. Maniho saw that they were carried back to their quarters, and the dead were taken to their burial vaults in a certain place within the city walls.

Pulling them aside, I then told Leahu and Maniho about my plan. They seemed concerned, but Leahu said he would support me in my decision.

He offered, "It was best for you to tell us, rather than go on your own without us knowing. This is not so we can talk you out of it, but so you will not go in your own strength without Ahueha. Now, we will support you in our prayers. It would have been most dangerous for you to go without at least one partner preparing the way with you in unified prayer. You will have both Maniho and me behind you."

Maniho nodded and said, "If you are ready, we will show you the best place to leave without being seen by servants or enemy scouts."

I went back to the room and finished dressing for the trip. I took the lifter and energy generator out to a porch at Maniho's residence. I heard the passionate prayers of the Kamikini in the square as I loaded up two laser cannons onto my shoulder gear along with the scope rifle and bullet pistol. In a front pack, I put several boxes of bullets and ten grenades where I would be able to get at them quickly. The Avenger's shield tied comfortably to my waist in front. The sword in its sheath swung over my back, the handle at my right shoulder and the blade end at my left thigh. I put on the infrared visor and helmet with heads-up display. That was the most armed I had ever been.

Before I left, Maniho advised me where to look first in Hekanalo for my family. Using thought commands, I lifted into the air and flew up over Kohilo. Maniho and Leahu were proceeding to the square to join the rest of the Kamikini who were already praying there. As I cleared the walls, I knew they could not see me, but I could see the army arrayed outside with my infrared visor. They formed a ring around the city. No Kamiki would be able to escape their morning attack.

Darkness lasted about 10 hours, so I needed to hurry. I made the trip to Hekanalo in about 10 minutes. I scanned the ground visually and with my sensor array as I went, seeing a few Hekanalo soldiers in groups along the way. There may have been more, but they were not visible to me. As I approached the city, I saw it clearly bedded down for the night. Only a few lights were on in the main streets.

I moved cautiously over the walls and circled the city slowly scouting out the arrangements. It was clearly a Kamiki city in layout. Based upon my intimate knowledge of the other city, I determined where the leader's residence would be. The jail off to the side of the residence looked occupied. I landed close by and gave the command that folded up the lifter onto the center of my back under the sword.

Guards sat at the door talking softly to each other. I approached slowly to be able to hear them. From a side alley about 15 feet away I turned my audio enhancer to a volume which made them sound like they were next to me.

The one to the left of the door said, "... as he told us. And that is why I don't like being left here. There is no action here. If the Kamikini stand between us and life forever, then I want to be one to take part in their extermination. I feel insulted to be among the few left behind."

The other one replied calmly, as if tired or bored, "You know someone has to stay here. The alien may come to attack our city while the others are away. All of our possessions he could destroy easily if we were all gone. Besides, in a few hours, every Kamiki will be dead. Then the general can set in motion his plan to get rid of the alien and his kind. As he said, 'We have let the alien become complacent with his strong weapons. We have his cherished ones now. We will let him have them back and think he is safe, then we will surprise him and kill all the aliens at once. Then we can live forever on this world until we can leave it.'"

"That all sounds good, Lamaki, but I think we should hit him at the same time we hit the Kamikini. I do not believe like you that the general must always be right. I would feel better taking care of a few things myself."

"That is dangerous talk, Wolohine. You will see General Anakuia is right. He has been right for over 200 years. Give him time to show his wisdom once again."

They remained silent for a while. Then Lamaki spoke again, "I am restless. Help me check on the prisoners and the alien machine."

At that I perked up. I flipped up my visor to adjust my eyes to the lights on the street. He got up and unlocked the door. Both of them went inside. I moved to the door and found they did not lock it behind them.

Stalking them carefully inside, I left the audio enhancer on to hear them. No voices. I went down the concrete hallway in front of me. After about 50 feet, I heard them in the back. I pulled out my pistol with suppressor and continued slowly that way.

At the end of the hall it branched to the left and right. To the right was an open door. I looked carefully inside and saw the sphere which my loved ones came in. There was a large outside door through which they must have brought it. The sphere looked charred and slightly misshapen. If my family had managed somehow to jump in spite of the explosion, then the jump may have been imperfect, injuring them throughout their bodies.

I wanted to get them away and see if the healing robot could help them. I suspected they were in agony when the energy source for their jump lost power at the last moment. Every hour without treatment made death closer. It sobered me to consider that some may have died already.

These thoughts fired up my anger. Anxious now to get to them, I turned and softly ran down the other way. Another door at the end opened up into a cell block. As I entered, the guards saw me and pulled their swords. Two quick shots felled them. It would have been more noble to use my sword, but time was short.

The cells ran along the left wall. I turned to search the cells to pull my loved ones out and be off. I wanted to get them out now!

Within the span of 20 seconds, I went from serious actions and immediate planning to almost total frustration. None of the ten cells had my loved ones! The first five cells contained Makura prisoners. The last five were empty. Where were they? I felt confusion and frustration mixed with my anger.

The Makurani prisoners were horrified to see me. Some backed away from the fronts of their cells and cowered against the back wall, moaning in disbelief and terror. I went to the front of the middle cell and stood back where all could see me. Spreading out my arms so they could see my weapons, I shouted, "Where are the aliens from another world?"

When none answered, I screamed louder, "Tell me now, or I will kill each of you right where you are!"

Again no one moved, and they became deathly silent, so I walked to the first cell and pointed the pistol at a prisoner. He screamed and yelled, "They are not here!"

"Where are they?"

"The general had a group of soldiers move them away from the city. He said you might come and try to get them like this."

"Where did he send them? Tell me now!"

"No one knows! He told only the group, so no one could tell you if you came!"

"Where is the general, then?"

"He is outside Kohilo. He also figured you would try to find him, so he is in disguise. He said he would look like any other soldier."

"Does anyone else know where my kind are?"

"Only those who took them away."

Complete frustration flooded over me. My anger was becoming so strong, I wanted to kill every Makura I saw just to get at this general, starting here. With exceptional restraint, I ask through gritted teeth, "How do you know all this, since you are prisoners in here?"

"No one was in here until he briefed us on his battle plans. We were all selected to go to Kohilo and did not want to go. Therefore, he had all like us put into this stockade until after the battle."

"Why did you want to stay in Hekanalo?"

He did not answer, but only looked at the other prisoners. They looked at him and none looked at me. I knew the answer. They did not want to be killed by this alien. A few days longer in a prison were better than certain death at the hands of a powerful and invincible enemy. And now this horrible alien threatened to kill them right here in the safest place in Hekanalo!

Unless General Anakuia skillfully planted them here, they had probably told me everything I wanted to know, although the answers were not what I wanted to hear. What did they have to lose? I did not press for more answers. I turned and left in a controlled rage.

I looked up and cried out, "Lord, if you want me to fulfill this horrible mission, please tell me where to find my family!"

Leaving immediately through the front door, I remembered their sphere. It might be helpful later. After going back to it, I opened the outside door. The Makurani had placed the sphere on a wheeled skid. The door was locked solidly. Some of my frustration enjoyed release blasting it with laser beams. A simple push opened the door. No one was inside.

123

I got inside the sphere and used screws and metal straps to fasten the lifter to a titanium support at one side of the doorway of the sphere. Testing it, I gave brain wave commands to rise up very slowly. I kept increasing the power command without success until I decided to try an assumption. The sphere has around 40 times my mass, so I told the command unit to assume the weight was in that magnitude. I ordered a rising rate of one foot per second. The sphere tilted slowly to where the side the lifter was attached to the framework was facing up, then it ascended at about one-half foot per second.

My assumption was close enough. The lifter was programmed initially for my body mass, but it could move much greater weights. I ordered it to increase speed until the sphere was well above the city, then I headed to my main shelter. I keep experimenting with the speed until we were traveling at 60 mph.

The power generated by the little energy generator on my back was amazing. At other times, I would have experimented with its capabilities. Now I wanted most to get to my shelter and then find my loved ones somehow.

It felt like hours getting there, but I soon unloaded the sphere near the shelter site. I maneuvered it between some trees where the bushes were high. I got out and covered it with tree limbs and bushes pulled out of the ground with the lifter's help.

I returned quickly to Kohilo. In two hours, it would be dawn. Perhaps I could figure out who the enemy general is and force him to take me to my family. God was granting me no other insight at that time. Trying to find them near Hekanalo at this point would leave the city of Kohilo as an easy target for the Makurani. I did not feel right leaving the Kamiki now, especially if there might be some chance of finding the general.

As I made plans, I realized my love for my own family and for Maurice's did not overpower my concern for the innocent at Kohilo. I could not leave so many who were unable to defend themselves against evil oppressors. They had already suffered so much, and I was now their official protector. Through legal ceremony, I had the right to defend them, and I kept reminding myself that I had the authority to take the initiative in vengeance. Besides, there was some hope I could find my own before the group hiding them discovered the battle results. "Provided I survive," I thought.

I arrived over Kohilo well over one hour before sunup. Using my visor, I slowly flew over the circle of enemy soldiers at 50 feet above the ground, flying in and around the trees. Any hint of activity and I stopped to hover and watch.

Two trips around the city revealed nothing. This was very frustrating. Up until now, events involving the Makurani had gone my way. Maybe not this time. They seemed surprisingly confident of victory.

When the faint light of dawn appeared on the horizon, the trumpeters give the wakeup call. Many were out of the tents immediately, having not slept well anyway. I rose to 100 feet to watch. As the rest come out of their tents, a soldier saw me and pointed at me as he loudly announced, "The alien! The alien!"

I tried to make out whether the soldiers appeared to give word to one particular person. They formed immediately into 20 companies of 125 soldiers, with no separate leaders standing out. Each company acted as if it needed no leader. *They must be acting upon pre-battle plans to keep me from finding the general. He is a brilliant chess player! Maurice would have a tough time playing against this fellow!*

Maurice's advice to protect my king came to mind. I decided to rise higher just before the nearest company of soldiers suddenly turned their crossbows at me and fired. Since I rose at the last moment, only those mis-aimed hit me. About 25 struck me on the way up and bounced off my armor. Their force pushed me sideways a little. About eight hit my helmet and dazed me for a second. A direct hit by several dozen might have stunned me. *Even now Maurice gives good advice!*

I hovered at 300 feet and reversed the amplification direction of the audio enhancer to use the miniature loudspeaker function. "People of Hekanalo, I am here to protect the Kamikini. I am now their Avenger. I bear the Shield and Sword of the Avenger."

I brought the sword out to show the soldiers on this side. They showed excellent discipline and remained quietly in their positions. I circled the city flying over the troops with my sword raised high, so all would be able to see it.

When I came back to the start, I gave these conditions, "People of Hekanalo, I will let you return to your city if you will do three things. First, turn your general over to me. Second, tell me where to find my family and friends. Third, stop this attack on the Kamikini and return to Hekanalo."

I circled the camp and repeated this on all four sides of the city to the soldiers. Then I circled the camp again with this message on each side, "Turn your general over to me now!"

By the end of my second pass, no one had moved out of formation. I waited a minute and made a third pass, saying to each side, "*Meet these conditions now, or you will die in this attack.*"

No one moved at the end, so I went to a point over the middle of the city about 500 feet up and waited. Hovering there I slowly rotated while holding up the sword to discern any effort to yield. They remained in formation.

A trumpet blared out a battle signal. The sound of 20 trumpets then filled the air from all sides.

I looked below to see the Kamikini still praying in the square. They looked exhausted right before dawn. Each was up and praying earnestly to the Creator. *Will this be the end for them? Can I alone stop this massacre of those who are unable to defend themselves? Can I stop an attack on 20 fronts?*

The sword went easily back into its sheath. I activated the visor's aids by thought to provide computer enhanced aiming for the laser cannons on my shoulders. The heads-up display estimated how quickly each company would be able to reach the wall out of my view when they started to run forward. The companies closest to the wall were on the north side. They should reach the wall in 15 seconds. The farthest from the wall were at the main entrance to the east. They should get there in 30 seconds. Not much time!

The first edge of a twin sun peeked over the horizon, and the Makurani shouted as one, moving quickly toward the walls. My plans would have to unfold as the attack proceeded. I aimed the cannons at two companies on the north side nearest the east corner. Painstakingly yet quickly, I wiped out both companies using a constant beam from each weapon, sweeping the advancing troops and cutting their ladders in two. This took about seven seconds.

I swung to the left to hit two more companies on the north side of the city. The others gained ground quickly. I swung to the right and managed to wipe out four more companies on the east side before they got to the walls. There were twelve companies left, and they were preparing to scale the walls.

I swooped outside the city to the north at a low angle and turned to face west. The soldiers in each company grouped together at the base of the walls. Starting at the northwest corner and swinging around the outside walls counterclockwise, I swept the beams over the soldiers climbing the walls and gathering below them. They were packed tightly at the ladder bottoms, so the lasers handled one company after another quickly. Soon only three companies remained at the southeast corner.

The three companies left had soldiers over the wall. A sweep of those outside caught 140 in the last three companies. The heads-up display said that left 235 who got inside. To defend the people in the square, I broke off this outside attack and went over the wall and inside the city.

The Kamikini were still there. *Why don't they take cover?* Also, I remarked to myself, "This is all happening so quickly!" But there was no time for analysis.

I suddenly realized the Kamikini were in the ideal place. They were the farthest distance from all the walls when in the square. The soldiers left can only come from the southeast quadrant, and the city has wide, main streets going east-west and north-south. In seconds, I was hovering over the southeast end of the square able to look down those two main streets.

When any soldier showed himself in the streets or in a building, I picked him off. The visor display showed me any soldiers in view and advised me of the thickest concentration when several were in view at once.

The Kamikini responded to my hand gestures to move to the northwest corner of the square. Most prostrated themselves, and all continued in prayer.

I moved down low, about 10 feet up. The visor computer had been keeping count. About 175 soldiers remained. None were advancing right then. They must have been regrouping and planning a special coordinated effort. Acting intuitively, I took the shield loose from my belt and held it in my left arm, putting that laser cannon in standby. The other laser cannon on my right side was still ready for action.

At the sound of a trumpet, dozens of archers appeared in windows, doorways, and the streets of the eastern side of the square. They let fly with their poison arrows at me. I held up the shield to deflect those coming at my head. Over 100 arrows hit at once, throwing me backwards a little in the air.

But this time I had expected something like that. I took aim immediately and fired the beam at the targets still exposed, even while I was floating backwards. The beams took out 23 before they finished watching me to take cover.

My rage was rising. Like a provoked moose during mating season, my main hindrance was trying to remain calm enough to be effective. I was remarkably focused.

Time for grenades. I hated to ruin the beautiful dwellings here, but life was much more precious. Giving the Makurani a little time to regroup near the front walls of the closest buildings, I set the grenades for different time delays of short duration. The infrared scanner showed the soldiers were mainly in three sets of buildings, so I set six grenades. Swooping quickly past each dwelling, I tossed two grenades into each. They went off before I was back in position at the center of the common.

These particular grenades were more powerful than I had expected. Also, the dwellings were flimsier than I thought. The blasts literally ripped the fronts off the buildings. Heavy debris struck me, and some fell on the praying crowd across the square. Dozens of soldiers were thrown out in pieces before me. The computer counted 132 killed in the blasts, unceremoniously treating some of the body parts as puzzle pieces put back together. Only about 20 soldiers remained.

No one revealed himself for some time. On a hunch, I motioned the praying crowd to the center of the square. The soldiers might have moved to the sides during the confusion. I showed them I wanted them to huddle up close, crouching behind the tables and other outdoor furniture there. I flew around them near the dwellings, inviting arrows and scanning with my visor. While I was flying on the south side, a group of archers appeared in windows on the opposite side. In one launch, they fired five poison arrows from each crossbow at the crowd.

I flew over and dropped a grenade into the building. Positioning myself more carefully, only a little bit of the heavy debris hit me, and some hit the close-by crowd. The visor counted 14 more dead soldiers.

Now only about six remained, if each company had exactly 125 warriors in it. At this point, there was a significant difference between 6 and 16 remaining. When no one attacked for a few minutes, I rose up high over the city to look. The visor picked up eight targets outside the city to the southwest. Using the zoom feature, I could tell they were fleeing.

Should I let them go? A debate raged inside my head. The answer was, "No." I soared past their location and swung around to face them. They tried to stop and fire at me, but they were quickly dispatched.

Nowhere in all this did Anakuia show himself. A quick flight along the outside walls with the visor turned on revealed all Makurani were dead. No one else was in range of my sensors.

I flew back to the crowd. The 70 arrows did not have full flying force because five flew from each bow at once. Only 18 struck a person. These were lying down and were dying slowly. One who took two arrows was nearly dead and beyond help. I flew into the residence and got my healing robot. I had programmed it ahead of time to make up several ounces of antidote in case it was needed.

The antidotes were injected quickly. Each would recover, although two would be quite ill for several days. I also used the robot to help three persons hurt by debris from the explosions.

Generals Maniho and Leahu advised their people to go cautiously back to the dwellings. They also sent assistants outside the city to check the outer walls for ladders to remove and destroy any that were left and to put out fires caused by the laser beams. Guards went and took positions on the walls as watchmen with trumpets to report any returning warriors. That night would see a bonfire for ladders in the square, and then the people would hopefully enjoy a night of rest.

The entire battle lasted only 25 minutes. The visor counted 2,502 Makurani killed. Only one Kamiki died.

I felt numb and nauseated. Maniho made sure I was all right. He instructed aides to bring food and drink for me.

Maniho grabbed me by the shoulders and said, "Friend, you must refresh yourself. After a personal battle such as this, the strain will have weakened you greatly."

Weary and weak, I replied, "Two thirds of the Makurani are dead, but over a thousand remain. My own are dying somewhere at their hands. Therefore, my battle is not over yet. The day has been long, but I cannot rest yet."

"My friend, you must! You will not be able to go on much longer at your present strength!"

We argued some more, and he finally prevailed upon me. His aides brought food and drink quickly, but it took me a few minutes to come down emotionally from the battle. The food and drink looked wonderful, but they tasted like cardboard and water. I forced myself to eat because I needed the nourishment.

I had not slept in over 24 hours, and the physical and emotional strain had been intense. Yet rest was not an option. I wanted to get back on the trail for my own people in case the group holding them might not have heard the results of the battle. Every hour might be critical.

Chapter 17: Keep Going

The pause to take some food and drink refreshed me. I ate a small balanced meal at Maniho's insistence, but then I wanted to press on to Hekanalo.

He said, "I only wish I could go with you to look for your loved ones, but my place is here with my people. Nevertheless, I want to help any way possible."

"Thanks, Maniho. This I must handle alone, although it is very lonely work."

Then I asked him, "Where do you think I will find my family and friends?"

He advised, "General Anakuia probably was here for the battle today. He would have stayed safely out of the way once the fighting began. He has probably sent word ahead to tell his forces what happened, using a courier. Now he is either returning to Hekanalo or is sending a force to attack again. You may want to watch for his troops when you go out."

Continuing his assessment, he advised, "Your loved ones are surely only a short distance out of Hekanalo. Anakuia would want to bring them quickly back when he saw you defending us. He hoped you would stand aside, but he always plans for each alternative. If he is returning there, then you can be sure they will be in or near the city when he arrives. He may have them killed, or he may let them live to try to bargain with you some more. He is a brilliant strategist who has often surprised me."

I said, "Do you know of a probable location where they may keep my people?"

"He would not risk you finding them in a dwelling which could be spotted and checked. They are probably in a tent or are hidden in caves or dense trees. Normally, 10 to 15 warriors would be guarding your six. Any group that size you find would be good to check out."

He added, "I have set up a hidden chain of my soldiers to listen for the trumpet blasts in and around Hekanalo. Although we cannot defend ourselves directly, we believe it is permissible to help you. Also, if you can show my people how to monitor those flying monitoring machines you have, then we could use the device you called a radio to let you know if we hear or see anything that is happening."

"Good idea. Please get me two or three of your assistants and bring them to my equipment room so we can do that."

We hastened to the equipment room, gathering the two assistants on the way. I showed them how to monitor the drones as well as how to use the small radios to talk to me. The range is over 50 miles, and so they would be able to easily communicate with me even when I was at Hekanalo or beyond. Maniho decided to use the radio himself and instructed the assistants to give him a report every 15 minutes or whenever they had something important to share. Then he would decide whether to radio me.

I discussed my plans with Maniho. The plans we made were to have his people send scouts out in all directions at least 5 miles from the city to warn of another attack.

I planned to fly over the area between there and the enemy city to check for troops. Then I would scout out the area around Hekanalo to look for small groups of troops who might be guarding my people. And if I could find Anakuia, I would capture him alive.

Maniho advised me to hide my weapons I had inside the city in case a small force of Makurani came to take them and use them against me. Most were attuned only to my hand grip or retinal scan, but not all. We placed them in a secret storage place he made in the last two years which the enemies had never found. If the Makurani found the location anyway, heavy locks and bolts would make them take precious time to break in, enough for me to speed back and protect the stash.

I went to my room and prepared to go out as planned. My gear contained some food and drink as well as the set of weapons I used earlier in case I wanted to scout around later at night. Maniho advised I take extra grenades, so I took 20. He and my assistants helped me to the front of the leaders' residence. I loaded up and received a report that the enemy seemed to be silent with their trumpets, and the drones did not show anything unusual. It did not appear they would re-attack soon. Their actions focused on their regrouping at home.

After hugging my Kamiki friends with their double shoulder squeeze and a smile gazing deeply into each other's eyes, I lifted off. I soared up to 2000 feet and proceeded at 100 miles per hour southwest toward Hekanalo. I used the visor and its heads-up display to watch for any troops. The only troops I saw nearby were Kamikini. If Anakuia was returning to his home, he hid well as he traveled.

In a half hour I approached Hekanalo for the second time. I avoided the city, not wanting them to see me. I stopped my approach to the city from five miles out and dropped to 250 feet up. I then circled the city in a spiral which decreased by one-half mile each time around. At 100 mph this took around three hours of strained searching and tense examination of every unusual object or movement. The visor picked up no warriors at all.

It was two hours before sundown. My spiral took me finally to the outside walls of the city. I passed around them at 500 feet up and 500 feet away from the walls. The streets were empty.

Their thoughts probably were, "The killer is near! Hide!"

When I was halfway around the city, a small contingent moved into the center of their town square. I radioed back to Maniho. He said the conversations picked up by the drones indicate they have seen me and expect me to come into the city. I told him of the contingent in the square. I decided that I needed to go down to them. He warned me to watch for a trick. I signed off and prepared to move in.

I pulled the shield into my left hand and energized the laser cannon on my right shoulder. With visor down and attention high, I lowered myself down into the square hovering a few feet above the ground about 25 feet in front of the contingent. A leader came forward to speak.

He said to me, "Alien, we have no quarrel with you. Why do you continue to destroy us?"

"You have continually attacked me and my friends, the Kamikini. So far, I have only defended myself and them. Furthermore, you have found my family and friends from my world and are keeping them from me. Return my own from my world."

"We desire to give you your own, but we fear you will only keep on attacking us until you kill all of us. Your own would like ..."

My radio burst into life. "Daniel, a trap! Leave now! Leave now!"

I gave the thought command, "Emergency rise now!"

Right before I heard the warning, doors to buildings to my direct left and right swung open quickly. Large arrow catapults were aimed at me and were quickly fired. Maniho was with his assistants who noticed the video on two of the drones that showed what was happening. One device was aimed straight at me and the other about 10 feet above my head in case I tried vertical evasive action. Each arrow was 15 feet long and heavy enough to severely bruise me if I took a direct hit against my armor.

I did not see either one out of the corner of my eye, since I had no time to look. The one aimed low came from the right and passed just under my feet. The one aimed higher came from the left straight at me. The higher one struck me waist high on the left side. Since I was carrying the shield of the Avenger in my left arm, it hit the shield and spun me around sharply to the left. I pirouetted like a rifled bullet as I climbed rapidly to 1000 feet and hovered there. The automatic functions of the lifter quickly ended the spinning.

My left arm and ribs felt bruised, and my left shoulder felt like the arm had been nearly torn off. The shield was dented, and I was very dizzy from the spinning. The adrenaline was flowing fast too. I was in pain but ready to strike back. Many Makurani had swarmed into the open to see if the alien had been mortally wounded.

I paused briefly to compose myself. Angry and hungry for a counterattack with real punch, I waited until the crowd in the square appeared to be at its maximum. Then I suddenly swooped down like an eagle on the village center. On the descent I took out five grenades. As at Kohilo earlier, I throw one into each of the four main buildings facing the square as I flew past. I climbed and dropped the fifth on the square itself.

I put the laser cannon on full steady beam and begin sweeping the city with its beam of destruction. Any sign of a soldier detected by my visor caused him to be picked off like an arcade target. Soon no one was visible, and the buildings on the square were burning. Anyone left must have fled or hidden deep inside a dwelling.

Seeing the leader's residence, I armed two grenades and dropped one inside the main entrance end and one inside the back porch. The blasts tore most of each end clean off, with only the center core still standing. One more descent with an armed grenade leveled it violently.

I was still terribly angry. I returned to the square and used my loud-speaker again. As I circled the square at 75 feet up, I shouted four times,

"Where are my people from my world? You continue to strike at me and try to kill me! I will level this city to the ground in five minutes unless you bring them to me! Send a messenger out into the central square to speak to me. If I hear no word, this city is gone!"

I had 12 grenades left and intended to use them all. After that I planned to laser beam the city until everything which could burn was on fire. Nearly everyone left in the city would die, and Hekanalo will look like yesterday's campfire.

A man appeared and moved to the center of the square. I moved closer and used my loudspeaker to inquire, "What is your intention? Have you decided?"

"I am the personal envoy to General Anakuia. Your own kind are in the city. If you attack us with explosives, they will die with us."

"Bring them out to me, and I will leave your city with them."

"If you will fly away for five minutes, we will bring them out to the square."

"Bring them out to the front of the city main gates. I do not want them inside."

"We will bring them to the square. That way we know you will not strike us again until you have received them."

"Very well. I return in five minutes."

At last I will see them! I pray they are alive and well enough to be healed. It will be so good to embrace them and touch and smell them! Oh, how I have wanted this! In less than five minutes we will be together again! My heart is jumping out of my chest. I can hardly wait.

I radioed Maniho and he heard my happiness. Then he cautioned me that Anakuia could be setting another trap.

"I don't want to hear that now! Why can't you just let me be happy to see them? Please realize how hard this has been on me!"

Maniho spoke calmly and slowly, "Daniel, I have seen the enormous strain you have felt. And you are exhausted. I too know such pain, only I must wait until I am dead or glorified to see my own. Anakuia knows you desire strongly to see them and that you are tired. Please proceed cautiously. He is a brilliant commander. He is also the most evil and malicious of all the Makura."

He continued, "Daniel, your drones have picked up a lot of chatter among the Makurani the last three minutes. Some war action has begun. We do not know what it is, but please be cautious. Anakuia does not have any regard for you or your own. He will use them against you as long as he can. Will you be careful?"

I paused to let his knowledge and his wisdom sink in. He knew well what was happening.

"Yes, I will be. And I am again sorry to have yelled at you. I know you understand my pain. Yet I do not want to lose a loved one while I act too slowly."

"Daniel, we continue to pray."

I listened to my heavy breathing for a while, then replied. "Thank you, my friend."

The agonizingly long five minutes ended. I moved quickly back to Hekanalo, still smoking from my earlier grenades. I moved carefully past the wall and flew over the buildings toward the square. As the square came into view, I saw stakes standing in the square, and six humans had been tied to them. Each looked too weak to stand. They were sitting or leaning against their ropes. Around them were 30 soldiers. Each set of five had his crossbow aimed at one human.

My emotions and thoughts were racing faster than ever. I felt almost like I did when I ran away. *I must not, I will not, collapse under this pressure they are placing me under!*

I came closer and called out, "Anakuia, you are obviously playing with my mind. But now I know your tricks. Release my own or be destroyed!"

The envoy shouted back, "Alien, for the last time, we will be done with the Kamikini. Your own will live if you do not attack my forces. Let us remove our enemies, then I will release these to you."

He added, "Alien, they are not well. Some look as if death is near without your help. Let us go and eliminate the Kamikini, and we will return and give these to you. The Kamikini are nothing to you, but they are our true enemies. These you see here are the only ones who mean anything to you. Surely, they are more important to you than strangers."

Just then I heard from Maniho. "Daniel, we are soon to be under attack again. One of our scouts was killed before he could alert us. Two others report now that Makura soldiers are within 25 minutes of the city, coming from the north. A large force, yet smaller than last time, is fast approaching us."

Maniho continued, "Our friend, you alone must decide what you will do. We are not of your kind. Your own are in danger. We are in danger. We pray you decide as the Creator desires. May your wisdom be greater than ever before. I will end our talk now so that you can decide and then act."

The radio went silent. I looked at my watch to see how much time I had. With tears in my eyes and looking up with a breaking heart, I prayed earnestly for wisdom and strength.

Is this what being in Gethsemane was like? How I wish this cup would pass from me. I knew I could not run away this time. One way or another, this "cup" would not pass until I drank the bitter fluid down.

I looked down at the humans who meant more than life itself to me. I saw my dear wife who had stayed with me through so many troubles on Earth. My two children had grown up in an Earth set upside down. How precious they have been! Maurice was my dearest friend. We were like Jonathan and David in the Bible. His wife and son were like my own sister and child to me.

I did not want to come too close. It probably would cloud my mind, and I knew deep inside of me that Anakuia had set another trap.

I turned the volume up on my loudspeaker so that my loved ones would hear as I said, "You evil beasts! Your armies are nearly ready to attack the Kamikini once more. Again, I must choose between thousands of innocents or my own whom I love. You give me horrible choices indeed!"

As I hovered there trying to decide, I could not help but use my visor to zoom in on Maurice's and my wife's faces. Aimee noticed where I was hovering above. I saw her speak softly to Maurice. They turned in unison and looked toward me. Each was smiling an old smile we had smiled at each other before. It was our signal. It said, "Don't worry about me. Do what is right. I will trust in God."

I raised my arm, and I saw them nod. The choice was made by those whose lives were more precious than my own.

I had about 15-20 minutes. I flew at 200 mph, much faster than I had flown before. The wind battered my suit and gear, but all the weapons hung on, and I could bear it inside my armor. I came near Kohilo in 12 minutes.

The entire force of 500 soldiers approached from the north side of the city, which made it impossible for me to detect them earlier. I slowed down to 45 mph at one mile out of the city and climbed to 1,000 feet. From there I eyed the front troops who were within 1,000 feet of the wall, so I fired both laser cannons at them. The suns were setting, so I would soon be able to see better with my visor on infrared than they could with their eyes. They must have hoped to slow me down after dark, not knowing I had such tools.

The 500 troops never got to the wall. The two laser cannons and four grenades completely wiped them out in less than five minutes. How foolish! I continued to survey the trees and flew several passes to get everyone.

I radioed Maniho about the short and successful battle. He said he would keep me posted if he got any information about another force showing up. Over 500 Makurani were still alive and waiting somewhere. I did not like having so many left over to deal with.

As I headed back to Hekanalo, a strong intuitive feeling urged me to swing north of Kohilo instead of flying straight to the other city. Since this was where the last group just came from, it did not make sense to me. After a couple of minutes, the feeling was so strong that I decided to double back and check it out.

I swung toward where the last battle took place. As I passed over the spot, I headed north at 250 feet above the ground at 50 mph. Around 10 miles from the battleground, the visor picked up another force of soldiers to the northwest.

Of course! Anakuia gave himself some insurance by sending the second group right along the tracks of the first. His plan would have worked, except for the one thing beyond reason - my inner guidance.

I hit this force like the last one, using the lasers and four more grenades. After several passes, the visor detected no movements among the soldiers. Again, I searched the area around them, then radioed Maniho and told him about this second battle. The visor mechanism counted exactly 1,000 killed in the two battles.

Now back to Hekanalo. Only a few Makurani were left now. Maybe Anakuia had delayed carrying out his threat. I would know in a few minutes, and each minute was too long.

Chapter 18: End of the Road

I streaked back to Hekanalo at 200 mph. No more soldiers appeared, and in a few minutes the walls came into view. Cautiously, I slowed down and moved over the city's center. It was twilight, so those below would still be able to see me. As I rose over the last buildings near the center, I saw my family remained unharmed.

The archers discovered I was overhead, so they reassembled quickly and aimed their arrows once again at the humans. We were in another standoff. I brought both laser cannons to bear on the archers. The shield was at my waist directly in front of me.

The computerized visor counted 3,632 Makurani dead since the first attack on Kohilo. From Maniho's earlier count, that meant only 46 were still alive. General Anakuia and his troops had come close to defeating me and Kohilo, almost catching me too far off-guard each time, yet I readjusted quickly and won each game played. I understood that the situation right then was most dangerous. He had his back against the wall. The 30 archers in the square were now the majority of his remnant. *Caution! I must "protect my king."*

I radioed Maniho. He may not be allowed to defend himself, but he could aid me. I described the situation and asked him to share his best advice.

He replied thoughtfully, "You are right. This is the most dangerous time. Anakuia will sacrifice any and all lives to protect his own. If he has any soldiers left, he will use every last one of them to stop you. If he can defeat you, he will embark on a one-man campaign to kill every Kamiki. To him, you and your own must also all die. Any human is a threat to be the actual Hakani. He will not let any of you live. He keeps them alive now only to draw you into another trap."

As I circled the square, I carefully considered my next moves. My family remained as hostages below. Up until that point, I had waited in a defensive posture for each of Anakuia's moves. It was time to take the offensive.

I called out on the loudspeaker, "Anakuia, how can we resolve this standoff?"

His envoy came out of the shadows and shouted back, "You have not met my conditions to release your own. You have killed nearly all my people. We should go ahead and kill these who are yours. You will kill us anyway. I have only to give the command, and they will die. Why should I let you have them?"

"Anakuia, I have acted only to defend the innocent ones whom you have attacked. Now you hold more who are innocent and you again threaten them. Perhaps we can yet make peace. Consider giving me my people, and I will let you keep what is left of yours if you solemnly promise to never again attack the Kamikini."

I flew the lifter down to the center of the circle of archers and close to the stakes, supposedly to listen better. I hovered at one foot above the ground.

The envoy looked at me from just outside the circle and stated, "Alien, we have no way to guarantee you will not attack us further... What?! .... What are you doing?! You monstrous creature!!"

When the envoy began speaking, I turned on the two laser beams and starting with the archers in front of me swept the beams through them. In case I was too slow, I had positioned myself in front of Maurice and our two wives to allow them the best chance to survive. The left cannon swept rapidly left in a 180° arc from straight ahead to behind me. The right cannon swept the opposite way. The 30 archers were caught off guard and were all dead in less than three seconds, too fast for them to flee or for the envoy to give the command to shoot.

Anakuia was obviously close enough to see the action. Of my five grenades left on me, I prepared four and then swooped around the square and dropped one in each main building facing the square. A few mangled soldiers and two arrow catapults were thrown out. Smoke and fire erupted on all sides.

Having no time to be delicate, I went back to my people and cut them loose with the laser cannons. I pulled ropes out of my backpack and wrapped them around their upper bodies. I cut off the ropes where needed and tied the other ends around the base of the lifter. I made the ropes into three lengths so they would not hang as one group together and hit against each other as we flew. Moving quickly as if all our lives depended on it, I finished in less than two minutes.

Turning around once, I swept the sides of the square with both laser beams to buy extra time. Rising slowly at first, I pulled us all into the air, then climbed to 500 feet and left the city. I set peak speed at 30 mph to reduce wind pressure and turbulence. At two miles out of the city, I landed long enough to tie them up better, then we were off again.

Maniho and I had made plans earlier in case I could get them out. I called over the radio, "Maniho, have you spotted any other enemy soldiers?"

He came back, "No. We appear to be safe for now."

"I have rescued my own and killed over 30 more Makurani. Have your medics arrived at my main shelter yet?"

"They are hurrying. They should get there in about 20 minutes."

"Please send a trumpet message to direct them to keep going without delay. I will be there at about that same time."

We had agreed to send a small contingent of his medics to the site with the healing robot. That would place two robots at the shelter where I took the second sphere. My hopes rose, although my people appeared so pale and near death, I was seriously concerned whenever I gazed at them. After a few minutes, most of them looked as if they had fainted or were unconscious, so I sped up and quit looking at them.

When I arrived at the site, the soldiers were uncovering the sphere. I had them get out the second robot immediately while I set up lights for us to see by. I had shown them earlier in the square how to use the healing robot and how to interact with it by voice commands.

I started first with my wife, Aimee, and I had them start with Maurice. I gave voice commands to both robots as the soldiers watched very closely and worked by my side. After 15 minutes, the robots had done all they could, and we moved to the next two. I let the medics handle them while I looked on. After 45 minutes, all the robot work was done.

The robots said they healed internal injuries and injected liquid food and medicines. The directions for follow up work given by the robots required attendants to be there at all times for help. The medics stayed and did as the robots told them.

I asked the robots if the humans would survive and recover. They told me Maurice appeared to have a 25% chance, and Aimee had 60%. The others had a 40% chance, except Maurice's daughter who had a 50% chance. I left them with the medics with instructions to use an extra radio of mine to advise Maniho of any changes.

I was soon airborne and flying back to Hekanalo. I calculated Anakuia and 12 soldiers remained, and the automatic system in my visor confirmed that. My life, the lives of my family and friends, as well as that of each Kamiki would never be safe until the Makurani were all gone. I knew I had to fly back and finish the job which was mine alone. It no longer felt so horrible. The Makurani had attacked the Kamikini and me so often that a fight to the death was inevitable. No Kamiki or any of my loved ones could be assured of living until every living Makurani was gone. Their numerous crimes and intentions to continue afforded no place for mercy. I seriously desired to complete the time of justice before dawn broke.

The lack of sleep was catching up with me. My last sleep had been roughly 40 hours ago. My breathing was labored, and my eyes felt extremely tired.

I gave my visor and lifter instructions to circle the city at 500 feet up and scan for soldiers. I would close my eyes and let the machines work for one pass at 2 miles out from the walls at 30 mph. That would take nearly 15 minutes. They were ordered to awaken me at the end of the pass or if and when they spotted a soldier outside the city.

Soon, the visor system awakened me when the pass by was accomplished. It was becoming more difficult to go on, but I could not rest yet. I checked with Maniho. He said all was well. I checked with the medics, and they said the same. The robots had overseen the medics giving food and other needs to the six patients.

I was ready to go into the city. As I descended, I asked Maniho his advice. He said, "Anakuia has never faced these types of setbacks before, and you have bested him several times now. Because of this, I cannot predict his precise reactions. However, be aware of his personality. He will sacrifice anyone for himself. The remaining soldiers are certain to do suicidal actions for the general if he asks them. Whatever it takes to kill you. Expect any underhanded or devious action. Be alert. Anticipate as best you can. Strike quickly when threatened."

He added, "Though we are exhausted, we know you are more so. We continue to pray for you until the enemy is gone forever. Hakani and Kamikini are one until you fulfill your task. May the Creator give you strength beyond measure."

"Maniho, I am feeling very vulnerable. Please comfort my own if anything should happen to me. And if they come back to health, ask them to finish the job that I have started."

He paused. Then he said, "We desire your continued life and health in victory. Nevertheless, I will do as you have asked."

I was then near one side of the square at 100 feet up. I increased the infrared detection level on the visor to pick up any residual air trails left by the remnant. The infrared strength of the small fires still burning in the city at this visor level was almost blinding. Nevertheless, I scanned the alleys and streets away from the square as I flew over them.

Halfway around the city I detected a trail which led back to the bombed main residence. It was fresh enough to be Anakuia and his remaining troops. I followed it to one side of the residence and saw it end at a door which went into a basement or tunnel.

I landed quietly at the entrance and took off the lifter, placing it on my back. Cautiously, I approached the door. I opened it ready to fire. No one was there. A trail of infrared led down the ramp to a landing from which the declining ramp went left and right.

I stopped and put one laser cannon, the lifter, and other gear under some debris. I put the silencing pistol with its 12-shot magazine in my right hand, with an extra magazine in my coat. Somehow the pistol felt strong and comforting. I left the laser cannon on my right shoulder with the shield on my left arm. The sword was on my back, and I had one grenade left. Without a backpack blocking its view, my visor was able to see all around my head and advise me of a sneak attack from behind or overhead.

I called Maniho and told him where I was. With his blessing in my ears, I took a deep breath and entered the doorway. It was dark both inside and out now.

With each step, I paused to see and listen. The audio amplifier was also set high. At the landing, I cautiously looked left then right. The infrared trail headed to the right. I heard only my own breathing and soft footsteps.

The ramp opened into a hallway 10 feet wide with five tall doors on each side, perhaps to large storage closets. The sides were of stone, and the ceiling was of some type of narrow grating with the roots of plants and dirt above. This area led to a narrow tunnel at the other end about 50 feet farther. A good place for a trap.

The visor heads-up display revealed a dispersion of the infrared patterns, so some Makurani were surely in the side areas waiting to surprise attack. I pretended to walk farther by placing my left foot forward and stepping in place slowly, but louder than normal. Left, right. Left, right. After about 15 fake steps, three side doors opened and six soldiers appeared with nets to surprise me in the middle, but I was not there. A rapid 12 shots from the pistol put them down.

I stepped over their bodies intuitively cautious of a second trap. Anakuia might set one right behind the first. After I replaced the pistol's magazine with the last one on me, I headed toward the end of the hallway. Two more doors opened, and nets are hurled at me. One fell behind me. The other covered my left arm and shield, but it did not entangle me enough to prevent my response. With six shots I put down four more soldiers.

There were now two soldiers left with Anakuia. *I sure hope Maniho gave me the right count.*

I proceeded at an even pace down the tunnel, shaking off the net. At the end of the tunnel, it opened into a much larger area. I slowly placed my head into the opening. My visor detected nothing. Infrared trails split up. There was one to each side and one a little stronger ahead. I backed up and let my intuition and logic take it in.

The room was by appearances a large underground warehouse. The ceiling must have been at least 50 feet high. I stuck my head back in and looked around for places where they could place an arrow catapult. Anywhere between the aisles would work. The aisles were 10 feet apart and ran off the center aisle left and right. Perfect for an ambush.

I moved quickly from aisle to aisle and looked down each. At the third aisle, my visor picked up something overhead. As I looked up, I saw a net coming down upon me. I fired several shots up through the net before it fell on me. With the laser cannon I rapidly and easily cut myself out. As I tossed it off, I saw a soldier running at me and nearly on top of me. He tackled me on my left side where I was holding the shield, and we fell down in a rolling heap. Rolling over further, I got my right hand free and fired two shots and heard an empty click. This soldier jerked and slumped on my legs.

I pulled myself up wearily and looked at the dead soldier at my feet. I saw nearby that another soldier, apparently the one who threw the net, had fallen from his perch above. My pistol had done its job on both, but the magazines were empty. I stuck the pistol inside a pouch, switched on the laser cannon on my right shoulder, adjusted the shield on my left arm, and then I went on.

Physical fatigue and mental exhaustion were catching up with me. Not much longer would I be able to continue without my body involuntarily forcing me to sleep.

If Maniho and the visor were correct, then only the general remained. But it was too early yet to assume that the count was correct. I checked each aisle as I passed. At the end of the room, a door led into another warehousing room like that one. As I passed through the door, the heads-up display revealed that the infrared trail split into two directions. At least one soldier was still with him.

I moved to my left and looked around the bins down the first aisle. I was too weary to use much finesse. Then I did the same with the second aisle. A heavy sword swung around and hit me squarely in the face mask.

The visor dropped out of infrared detection and my eyes suddenly had trouble seeing in the dim light of the underground warehouse. I fanned my laser around the area in front of me. When no one struck me again, I removed the visor for unhindered view and surveyed the area. In the dim light, I saw there was another soldier dead at my feet, sliced up by the beam. Bins and stored goods were on fire in several places.

The visor had been struck in the exact place where it was vulnerable. The blade hit a crack and sunk into the control wiring. I pulled the sword out of the crack in the visor and left it and the useless pistol on the floor. I had a dim level of light and needed to be able to move freely. My weakened body could not handle much weight right then anyway. The audio enhancer was part of the visor and also not working, so I tossed it down on the floor. My armor was fine, but my weapons were nearly depleted.

Then it fully dawned on me that only one foe remained. Hope and fear arose within me in an odd mixture. The hair on the back of my neck stood up. Soon I be face-to-face with the one person who had been behind all of the evil on the days I had known here. He was no less frightening to me than Satan himself. Without the knowledge of the rightness of my quest and the superiority of my equipment even then, I would have been tempted to flee in terror.

Chapter 19: No Pawns Left

I knew I could not run away then. I wanted to, actually needed to, end the nightmare, and I had to end it right there. In this game of chess, it was now king against king and, unlike in chess, there would be a checkmate. This time, we could not reset the board to play again. One of the kings must die. No more games would be played, ever.

I moved slowly down the center of the main aisle so he would not be able to do as the last soldier did. I checked each aisle left and right. I reached the dead end, but nothing moved along the way. I turned and paused, then I went even slower and more cautiously back to the front. I tended to stay closer to the left side on this pass.

At the second aisle I saw nothing again. As I passed the opening, a heavy sword suddenly arced at me from the left. I instinctively turned to face it. As I did, it hit me on the right shoulder. I backed away fast and trained the laser cannon in that direction and fired the beam. At least I tried. It did not fire. The blow pinched the cables against my armor and broke the connection to the generator.

With no time to repair it, I tossed it down and reached for my next best weapon. Aware that I had no other Earth weapons on me now, I had to pull the Sword of the Avenger from my back. The general heard the swish as it came out of the sheath and realized all my magnificent tools were gone.

"So, Alien, we now stand on equal terms," he said from the shadows. "And at last we meet!"

Soft boot steps from down the side aisle come closer to the center. My last and most terrible enemy on this world was about to face me. Both horrible dread and deep curiosity flashed inside me.

He stepped out of the bin's shadows. A more beautiful creature I had never seen. This creature-person which was beyond sexuality, neither male nor female but with the appearance of both beautifully mingled. "He" removed a jeweled helmet and displayed a full mantle of hair which any blonde beauty on Earth would be proud to have. His face was so fair and robust I was unable to decide whether I was beholding King David's Absalom or a goddess from ancient legend.

I continued to survey the archenemy who had taunted and tricked me so many times. Here he was. He was well over 6 feet tall and very muscular for a Makura. His skin was beautifully polished brass, a lovely combination with his flowing hair. His red and gold outfit included many medals and ribbons of brilliant colors, as well as insignia of high rank. How could this beauty be the enemy I had sought to destroy? Inside this artful exterior was there a sinister heart? Pure beauty and pure evil mixed into one person?

Still aware of danger, I looked and saw he had only a sword and no shield. And what a beautiful sword! It was rivaled only by the Sword I held. Then, I noticed his disarming smile in the dim light. He seemed no more capable of evil than my brother or my friend. He laughed robustly with a mellow tenor voice. He looked at me with contempt, but it sounded as if he was only sharing a joke with me.

He began to taunt me, saying, "Now you must use tools which you do not know and by which I have lived for much longer than many of your lifetimes. I am the greatest sword bearer on this world. Maniho was my closest equal, and he cannot use his now."

He tossed his ceramic sword around in his hand as if he grew up sleeping with it and continued without pausing, "All of your gallant efforts only to die at my hands. When I am done with you, I will search to find your own kind whom you worked so hard to rescue. I will kill each one of them. Then I will kill every Kamiki until I am the only one left on this dying world. Someday others will come to this place and I will make friends and leave with them. You see, I live forever until another who has knowledge of the Creator kills me on this world. If I ever leave here, I can never die. I will be immortal. Ahueha created the glorified ones so that even he cannot kill us elsewhere."

At that thought he laughed heartily as one savoring a sure and sweet victory after all seemed lost.

I stirred my courage and replied, "It is said in my world that a journey of a thousand miles begins with the first step. It also ends with a last step. I look like your first step, but you are instead my last step. I will start another journey after this. I am Hakani. You are my final act of justice for the Kamikini. Your road and mine both stop here."

He stopped smiling broadly and with a slight wisp of a smile, he condescendingly replied, "Come now, Alien. Surely you know by now when you are boasting beyond measure. We meet with equal weapons now. Your special advantages are gone. The weapon in your hand is one never before wielded before me by one so inexperienced as a warrior. You will not be able to land a single blow while I slice off pieces of your body until you die of blood loss."

His words were chilling. Knowing I still add my armor and my hope, I asserted, "Let us finish this, then, Anakuia. I have the blessing and destiny of Ahueha on my side. You have now only yourself."

"Ah, Alien, do you still boast? Can you not understand that this is the end only for you? You see, I have stood at the side of Ahueha. What you would desire to know about him, I have seen with my eyes and heard with my ears. Yet unlike you, I know his prophecies are only fulfilled when they are realized successfully in the physical realm. Until then, they are only his wishes. Today, I will fulfill my own prophecy, not that of Ahueha and the Kamikini."

With that, he pointed his sword at me and said solemnly, "I prophesy that I will today end your life, and Anakuia will live forever." He then opened his arms wide and laughed again.

Seeing he was at ease, I charged and swung at his midsection. His sword met mine easily, and I stumbled past, stopping several yards past him.

"I see, Alien, that you would try to even up the scales with surprise. However, the surprise will be yours. For now, I will toy with you. When I am ready, I will end this game with one blow. It will be a pleasure to see your head rolling across the floor."

He continued in a thoughtful tone, "But first, I would like to know some things about this Earth you come from. Is this where Apaliani now lives?"

Amazed, I asked, "Do you mean the senior devil over the world I come from?"

"Of course! I last heard from him almost 10,000 years ago. We were separated in the great civil war in our exalted realm at that time. He was the leader of the movement to run Creation as a democracy and not a kingdom. I was his prime associate. We could enlist only one-third of the subjects and, though we fought valiantly, we were divided into 2 groups and defeated outside that realm in this lower dimension. Most of those in the movement ended up confined in exile to a small planet with Apaliani and the smaller remainder back here with me on our pre-exaltation world."

"Before we go on, let us sit. Here is a stool for you." He scooted a wheeled stool over to me, then sat on a similar one himself.

Hesitating, I asked, "Are you not anxious to end this standoff? My duty is unfulfilled until you are dead, and you cannot rest until I am likewise."

On a hunch, I sensed he was off guard and threw my sword at him. While hardly looking at it, he used his sword to stop it in front of him in midair, twirled it around his a few times, then tossed it high in the air back to me, so that I could grab it by the handle without moving a step. No other Makura showed such incredible skill. How could I possibly best him? The hope within me said it could only be by "luck" in the power of Ahueha.

"My young friend, you are impatient." He smiled and gestured to my stool. "I am eons old. I have been back on this world nearly 10,000 years, and you have only been expected for the last 40 years, the total time since you were born. A few more hours or days are nothing to me."

Shocked by such a vast amount of time, I sat down heavily on the stool. I informed him, "I will speak with you for a while, but then I must finish my mission. I cannot rest until then, and I am weary now."

He continued, "Please humor me and let us share a few things about our worlds now. Tell me, is Apaliani truly on your world?"

"The senior demon over our world is called Lucifer, Satan, and Apollyon. His main aim is to destroy my kind. He desires to set himself up on the throne of God, your Ahueha, to receive the adoration of all creation."

"And why is that?"

"First, give me some more history of your battles in the past. Then I will tell you more about my world."

"Very well. The battles you are most interested in are those which ended with my army being sent back here, and Apaliani sent with the greater number there. Basically, the beings with Ahueha attempted to force us all back here. Here our powers are limited, and we are potentially mortal. On any other world we would live forever. Here we are able to live forever, unless another like us intentionally causes our death. Somehow, Apaliani was able to escape the trap to be sent back here, but some of us could not. His forces will live forever, but I cannot truly do so unless I leave here. And that will not happen until every Kamiki is dead, and your type along with them. But tell me, has your race existed for billions of years, and do you also become exalted as we?"

I replied, "Some believe our race has existed for millions of years, but those who trust in God's written revelation believe we were created by Ahueha only since about 10,000 years ago. At this point, I believe we were created after Apaliani came to Earth. Apaliani deceived the first two humans and gained control of the Earth. Because they turned away from Ahueha, the whole human race was doomed to death. Then Ahueha came into our world as one of us 2,000 years ago to die in our place, regaining rightful parental relationship to us and regaining control of the Earth. Those who side with Ahueha will live forever, and those who do not will end up with Apaliani. Apaliani is scheduled to be eternally punished, and all who followed him will also know everlasting suffering."

As I told this story, his face changed from confident serenity to quiet horror. He stared at me for some time, then said, "It then appears the only hope for Apaliani or for me is for us to be reunited and leave for other worlds. If I leave this one, and he leaves that one, then we will be free of the controls Ahueha has on us. Here I am mortal and limited. There he is also constrained."

He looked at me and suddenly laughed heartily. "Now I see! Ahueha has always allowed us who oppose him a way to win! His foolish tenderness never ceases to amaze me. My alien friend, you have provided the way! When I have disposed of all who have the breath of Ahueha here, I will find and study the equipment you brought here. I will use your radios to contact Apaliani on your Earth. Then we will study your traveling equipment on both ends until we can do the same thing. We will travel to other worlds and be free of our mortality. We will then grow in power and reach until we rule every other corner of the universe. Nothing will be impossible to us!"

I was suddenly glad to tell him, "My home base on Earth is destroyed! You will find no help there."

Condescendingly, he asserted, "Ah, my friend. You forget. Apaliani and I have plenty of patience to search out every scrap of data. We can probe the minds of your types on Earth, check other places where you have lived, scan every piece of paper and equipment. It may take a few months or even years, but we will be able to finally make it work. As for me, I will no longer be bound in my understanding of technology after the last Kamiki falls. My knowledge will grow like a sunrise emerging into full daylight."

He stood abruptly. "I must now continue my quest. Though I have much time, your story tells me Apaliani may be running out of his. Prepare to die, Alien."

With a yell he rushed at me, delivering a blow taken by my shield as I raised it reflexively. As he was earlier, I was caught off guard by our battle resuming so suddenly. The blow knocked me sideways off the stool and nearly put me on the floor. His strength was much greater than any of his soldiers that I had encountered there.

I lowered my face guard, locked it in place, and swung back at him. He easily deflected it, following the deflection with a countering blow on my right arm as my sword arced past. *He is so quick!* Struck with surprise that my arm did not fall off, I almost caught him unaware as I brought the sword back from left to right. He let me swing wildly past, then slammed a blow against my armor on my left leg before I could lower my shield.

"So, Alien, you have armor which is invisible in this light. Never mind. I will bruise you until you stumble in defeat."

We continued and I tried to strike at him without even one blow landing. Only my armor kept me from being cut apart. Many hard slows struck my body as I was helpless against such an expert. He was able at will to strike me above and below the shield on my armor. Each blow was hard and bruising. Once or twice I managed to deflect a blow of his. No effort of mine even came close to touching him. I could not even graze his uniform.

At one point, I felt a surge of hope as I managed to break his sword with a hard blow. He smiled and then hit my sword in such a way that it popped out of my hand and into the air. He grabbed it and tossed his half-sword back to me.

The fight continued and lasted for only a short while. My arms, midsection in front and back, legs, and head had taken dozens of bruising blows. Finally, my bruised left arm was unable to keep the shield up, and he struck me repeatedly all over. Blow after blow until my already weak body could stand no more, and he knocked me into a collapsed heap on my knees. He continued pounding until I could not even kneel, but lie helplessly flat on my back, hardly feeling the blows. He saw that I was powerless to even lift the sword anymore and lay nearly unconscious. He knocked it out of my frozen hand, and then he stood over me gloating.

"Now, Alien, I will remove your armor and strike the final blow of your mission. All was in vain! You have failed! You will die in the knowledge of your failure!"

He smirked and let out a chuckle, and this built up to loud roars of sheer pleasure, as I lay on my back numb with great pain, looking up at him. Half-conscious and with tears of despair rolling down my cheeks, I suddenly remembered I had one more option, the last grenade that was on me. As he laughed freely while wallowing in his great victory, I dragged it out from the bottom of my front pouch with my stiff and twisted right hand. I armed it with the only strength left in my arms and dropped it to roll toward his feet, my head and arms falling back down limp upon the floor.

He felt something touch his foot and glanced down as he continued his celebration. In a flash he stopped abruptly as he realized what I had done. He looked into my blurred eyes and screamed, "NOOOOOOOOO!!!"

The grenade flashed.

Both our journeys ended.

Chapter 20: After Hakani

A bird sat on a low branch in a tree singing its morning praise songs. It tilted its head and opened its beak wide like an opera singer exulting in the featured solo of his performance. Nearby, others joined in the joy of the morning. The choir had a richness not felt since eons ago. The last days had been unique.

The trees stood tall beside the stream flowing between the trees. The stream was full of water drops giggling as they ran and jumped on their way to the sea. They laughed and sang to each other and to anyone who listened, "Free. Free. All are free."

The stream flowed on by a tall city wall. Behind the wall a city was noticeably at peace. The people's faces radiated with happiness and pleasure. Greetings were warm and mellow, as if a great holiday had come. At times, a person looked up and uttered joyous praises with tears. No one had worked for five days. They had been enjoying a holiday week of celebration.

At the city's far end was the residence of the leaders. There the mood was a little more somber. Inside, a man was lying in a room with a machine hooked up to him. He was unconscious. Aimee Davidson and Michelle Monterre came again to check on him and inquire of his condition. The lead medic said, "I do not know for sure. Your healing machine says he has a chance but slim. About 30%." They had worked hard to learn the Kamiki language and understood well what he said.

The ladies went outside and told the three teenagers what they heard. All were thoughtful and quiet. The two ladies consoled each other with reassuring and kind words and gentle touches. The teenagers looked at each other and tried to act nonchalant. Then they sauntered over to the ladies and all shared a silent group hug. Wet eyes and breaking hearts. No men from earth were there to stand with them. And no words were spoken as they let go of their embrace.

Michelle said, "Let us leave here and visit General Maniho. Perhaps he will advise us how to pray or tell us something we can do."

They all nodded and followed her through the halls to his study. Along the way to the residence servants stopped and bowed their heads in respect. At the study, Maniho's door was open. Seeing them waiting there, he stood and motioned for them to come in and sit down.

Michelle said in Kamiki as she sat, "General Maniho, is there anything we can do for him? He has lain there for nearly five days. His chances for recovery are still slim. We want to do something. We have been praying along with your people each day for several hours, and God, Ahueha, has not healed him yet. We are losing hope."

Maniho smiled and took both Aimee's and Michelle's hands in his and squeezed them gently. He softly reassured, "As long as he lives, there is hope. Ahueha knows him and loves him. Keep praying and hoping. If the focused praying for prolonged periods becomes too hard, then reduce the length of time and go about your other actions with the prayer always in your heart. He hears you in your prayer closet as well as in your chapel. The hurt in your heart is a prayer. He feels all your pain. Let him act on his pain which you share."

The welled-up pain gave way to tears. The two ladies leaned forward and wept as Maniho held their hands. He squeezed their hands and respectfully placed them back into their laps as they continued to release their sorrow.

An assistant came to the door a little later, saw what was happening, and motioned to Maniho. He went over, and the assistant whispered in his ear. Maniho gathered up the teenagers quietly and herded them under his arms to outside the study.

The medics were waiting there and became suddenly excited. One blurted out, "He is stirring! He is still unconscious, but the machine says he is now only sleeping and will recover! He may awaken at any moment."

Maniho ordered his assistant, "Let the ladies know. They will want to be with him."

The teenagers and the ladies came running up and entered the re-covery room. One lady went to each side of the bed and held his hand. Then they sat and waited.

Through the night, they held his hand, walked the floor, hugged each other, cried tears of hope, and cried tears of concern. They spoke to the teens outside, sleeping on cots to be nearby. They spoke to the Kamikini who waited. They all waited. Sometimes he stirred, but he kept sleeping.

One hour after dawn they sent for breakfast. As noon approached, they lay their heads on the bed and rested. Michelle then felt something in her hand.

"Aimee, wake up! I felt something!"

Aimee stood and looked at his eyes. She perceived a slight flicker of eyelash and her heart jumped into her throat. A few more flickers and his eyes opened. He looked at her weakly, breathed deeply, and smiled!

She and Michelle stroked his head and Aimee said, "We thought you would die! But now you are back!" Tears and joy overwhelmed her ability to say any more.

He tried to speak. The words came slowly as raspy and feeble, like a forced whisper. "Wife.... Sister.... Good... see you.... Maurice... chil-dren... all right?"

Aimee said, "Yes, they are all right. Maurice was injured the worst and is bedridden for now. The rest of us have only minor bruises now and are fine. They say Maurice will be able to walk again in a few days."

Relieved, Daniel settled back and cried big tears of joy. Too weak to move, he let them flow down his cheeks. Aimee and Michelle lovingly wiped them off. Feebly he spoke, "I thought... I was dead.... After all the hardship... I thought I was through... But I knew... everyone else ... would be safe...And now... here... I am with you."

Aimee half lay on the bed and looked at Michelle. Both had streams of tears for him. They knew his emotional suffering had been intense. But they also knew that he would live. And in time, love surrounding him would erase most of the pain.

He went back into the sleep of the severely injured. They checked the healing robot. It said he could be expected to fully recover, although some injuries might take months to heal.

The next day at early morning, he stirred again. Aimee had refused to leave his side. Michelle had joined her and was watching while Aimee slept. As she noticed him stirring, she awakened Aimee. Straightening herself up and walking closer to the bed, Aimee looked down on his tired face.

I opened my eyes and looked up into Aimee's face. She looked so tired, but how beautiful she still looked! Those lovely blue eyes and golden hair that filled the screen of my world so many times. I reached up weakly with my right arm and tried to draw her to me. She read my desire and leaned down.

Those wet and tender lips touched mine again after so long! My heart was bursting. Her tears and mine washed my face.

Michelle leaned over and hugged us both, and we gladly shared the hug. She said, "I'll leave you alone now. I need to check on Maurice, anyway."

I pulled Aimee down on the bed beside me with my right arm lying under her neck. Aimee put her arm and leg gently across me and nestled up to my side.

I smelled her hair and felt my arm around her back. I kissed her forehead and rubbed her shoulder with my hand. I started to reach over with my left arm, but it did not move. It felt mostly numb.

As I held her, she talked to me softly for a while. Then we made sure I was comfortable, and she fell asleep next to me. Later, she got up, and I told her about the problem with my left arm.

The medics checked the healing robot, and it said I had a temporary paralysis due to the explosive shock. The left leg was also weak but should recover faster. Weeks of physical therapy needed to be endured for complete restoration of the use of the arm. It was good to discover that all other bodily functions were in good condition but needed strengthening. When I was able to eat, the machine unhooked me to stop the intravenous feeding.

When I awakened the next day, we began the recovery process. I started eating simple foods and sat up for a few minutes at a time.

Two days later, Maurice walked with a cane to see me. We held hands and shed tears. No words. Just smiles and squeezed hands at first. After he sat down in a nearby seat, I told him and Aimee a few details of the time I spent here while they were injured and captives of the Makurani. Still weak from the many days in bed, I tired quickly.

Three days later after taking a short and slow walk, I told Aimee about the showdown with Anakuia and about how I thought that using the grenade would be sudden death for me as well as him. It was a painful and embarrassing memory. She went and brought Maniho and Maurice to also listen as I told of the last hours of the struggle.

"Before I start, I must ask Maniho, how did you find me to bring me back here?"

Maniho answered happily, "When we did not hear from you, I sent a fast team to find the underground warehouse entrance you radioed about before you went in. They found the entrance filled with dirt from the grenade blast. As they searched further, they saw a large hole in the ground. The grenade blast blew off the roof of the warehouse which had been a layer of dirt three feet thick. They found you in your armor pushed over to one side of the room. You were barely breathing. All they could find of Anakuia was some mangled pieces of flesh and bone. The Sword of the Avenger was in one piece but badly mangled. We also found the Avenger's damaged shield nearby."

I interrupted, "He was holding the Sword of the Avenger at the moment of the blast. I was holding his sword which I had already cut in half."

He nodded in surprise then continued, "They brought you back to here in a stretcher with the weapons of the Avenger. We carefully removed the armor and had the medics you trained use the healing machine immediately. You do not know how glad we are to have you alive. We want so much to honor you. You are Hakani, and our Avenger is the victor!"

With that he stood and held out his right arm toward me with the palm down. It was a Kamiki salute. I held my right hand out toward him palm up to return the salute and said, "By the sheer grace of Ahueha, I am here. At the end, any of the blows from Anakuia could have finished me. Let me tell you, Maniho, about your great enemy and Anakuia's last moments."

I then hold them about the final trip to Hekanalo. That I could not even put a glancing blow on Anakuia fascinated him.

Politely interrupting at one point, he told the others, "Daniel and I had determined that Ahueha had given him a power to kill a Makura with even the lightest blow if the other one had something called "metal" pierce their skin. So, Daniel affixed some metal from his supplies to the tip of the Avenger's sword. If Daniel had been able to just graze Anakuia's skin, that monster would have died instantly. And yet Daniel could not even touch him!"

When I told about Anakuia's final words and the grenade, they were awed. I tried to be undramatic and factual, but they were all moved to stunned silence. We all sat in silence for a minute, then Maniho asked my leave and exited quietly. Aimee came to lie with me as Maurice also left quietly. Maurice touched my arm as he went by. A tear flowed down his cheek when he passed slowly through the doorway. My own tears started to flow again. Only Aimee remained, and she spent the night.

Over the next three weeks, Maurice and I both improved exceptionally each day. I was getting around with a slight limp, and he was nearly up to normal speed. My left arm was rapidly improving. I was able to hold objects in my hand and even raise my arm out to the side for a few seconds at a time.

Maniho sent a messenger to ask Maurice and me to come to his study. When we arrived, he asked us to sit down. After a bit of small talk, he shared why he asked us there.

"Leahu says he has received a word from Ahueha. The time to honor Hakani and his friends has come. We are arranging a ceremony in the square for this evening. Please carry the mangled Sword and Shield of the Avenger. Please also bring your loved ones with you." Seeing my reluctance, he added, "Please do this for Ahueha and for us."

We agreed on the time and proceeded to prepare ourselves and our families. At the appointed time of two hours before sunset, we met in our finest earth clothes at his study. Maniho and Leahu were waiting for us.

Chapter 21: Honors and Celebration

Maniho and Leahu stood as Maurice and I and our families entered Maniho's study. They greeted us and then escorted us out of the study. As we passed through the halls, we heard the sounds of an honor guard forming ranks outside. Maniho positioned us in the places of honor with the one hundred soldier escort leading us like royalty to the square.

As we entered the square from behind the crowd, every other Kamikini went to one knee and bowed toward the same platform at which I received the Sword and Shield of the Avenger. The guard detail preceded us to the front. Maurice and I followed, then our wives and children. Maniho and Leahu brought up the rear.

Attendants led us to our seats on the platform. Leahu proceeded to the front central position while Maniho sat between Maurice and me.

After having them stand, he addressed the Kamikini and said, "Beloved Kamikini, we have come to honor the Hakani which the Anakela foretold. Daniel came from his world to ours without knowing he had a moment of destiny here. Not a person of warfare on his world, he nevertheless fulfilled the purpose for which Ahueha sent him."

"Though he has said little about it, we know he intended at the end to kill himself along with Anakuia so we and his loved ones might live. Anakuia died, but Ahueha has let Hakani Daniel live. Bless Ahueha and his Hakani!"

The Kamikini broke into shouts and applause for several minutes. Then Leahu raised his hands and they slowly became quiet. He said, "Now is war ended for the Kamikini. We have no more need for weapons. Let the Discard begin!"

He turned to me and said, "Would you please be the first by tossing the Sword and Shield of the Avenger beside this stage."

I moved to the side on the audience's left. Holding the Sword and Shield high, I faced the crowd. They saluted me, then I turned and tossed the useless weapons down.

Leahu and Maniho then quickly and joyfully threw their knives, swords, and shields on top of my former weapons. The Kamikini filed by the side and happily added to the pile of discarded weapons by throwing theirs on top. After fifteen minutes, a huge pile of weapons lay beside the platform, and no Kamikini was armed anymore. The air was rich with silent joy.

Then Leahu stood again and said with unrestrained happiness, "We have not played the praises of Ahueha since our loved ones died." Spreading his arms wide, he continued, "With the enemy defeated and no more war, let the music now spring to life again!"

Each Kamiki reached to his side and lifted a musical instrument. There were horns and ceramic cymbals. Some had drums. Others had stringed instruments like violins and cellos and harps. When each had his instrument in place, Leahu lifted his arms again and conducted a symphony as beautiful as any waltz from Earth, yet more majestic.

We from Earth had never heard such lofty and inspiring music. Every emotion stirred. Our hearts lifted into worship of the Creator. We also knew him as a man and as our Lord. Our spirits moved us to our knees. Looking up, Maurice and I and our families worshipped God as never did before on Earth.

The symphony reached a forceful and emotional climax finished with timpani like drums and gongs. We and the Kamikini were speaking out our praises to God, to Ahueha, to him who was, who is, and who is to come. To Almighty God, the Lord, the King, the Father, we delighted to give our adoration and worship.

After about an hour, we sensed a calm come over all of us. We began to descend into quietness and let our singing hearts continue to praise as our voices become still.

Suddenly, a brilliant light broke out at the back of the platform. We hurried to the front edge of the stage and looked back at it. An archway opened up before us. It was nine feet high and six feet wide when it finished growing. Two Anakelani in white robes and wide golden belts stood in the doorway side by side. They stepped out onto the stage and then to both sides of the opening facing us. Each raised a sword high to the side away from the door.

Their skin shone like fire. The swords were as bright as suns. Their shields held waist high looked like sparkling diamonds. Through the opening, we saw a field of multi-colored flowers with a high crystal city in the background. A figure dressed like these others was walking toward us through a path among the flowers. Soon he came through the archway and stopped. He was as bright as the Anakelani, but deep love and fearsome power seemed intermingled in him.

We were awed and afraid. All of us had gone to the ground prostrate. Even the Kamikini had never seen this being. Could he be Ahueha in material form before us?

The figure spoke in a voice which was as loud as a choir but sounded as gentle as a mother's whisper. "Maniho and Leahu. Daniel and Maurice. Come to me."

When we hesitated, he lowered the volume to that of a normal voice, "Do not be afraid, but come."

We all moved forward and fell on both knees before him. He turned first to the two Kamikini, Maniho and Leahu. "I am most pleased with each of you. You and those with you of the Kamikini are the capstone of a glorious race which has been before my throne since time began. The construction of a building with living stones of Anakelani is nearly complete. When the last Kamiki comes to be with me, the building will be finished in all of its glory and beauty. From this point on, the final remnant of the Kamikini will be glorified quickly, and the last ones will come home to be with me as predicted. The last few will come to be with me at ten years from the very hour when Daniel arrived. Leahu, you will go with me now. Maniho, you will follow in a few months, after you have prepared those under your care."

He moved forward and placed his right hand on my head and his left on Maurice's. He said, still in Kamiki, "Your time as warriors in the tools of the flesh is over. I give you from now on my full power and protection. When the time is right, I will send you out together into the Earth along with an elect group to proclaim the truth of the end of the present kingdom there. No one can touch you to harm you during that time. Then I will hide you and your loved ones until your last days. Be wise and faithful to me from this point on. Tomorrow morning, an Anakela will tell you more. Then you will return to your world. Now, Daniel, look at me."

I looked up at him. He moved his hands to my shoulders, then smiled at me and said in English, "Well done in this task here, my faithful servant."

I blurted out, "My Lord, I felt so inadequate in this task. I do not feel I deserve this praise. I doubted you so many times."

He assured me, "Few tasks are without doubts and fears. You decided several times as I did that night in Gethsemane to follow the Father's will in spite of your unknowns and desires otherwise. You did all I could ask of you. You allowed me to use you as I chose. You did well, and I am quite pleased."

He turned and spoke the same first phrase to Maurice. Maurice said to him, "Lord, I did so little. While my friend struggled here alone, we were unable to help. We were even a burden to him when he came. How can you praise me for that?"

Looking into Maurice's face, he touched his teary cheek and smiled warmly at him, telling him, "Maurice, like Daniel, you did all I asked of you. I was free to use you as I chose, and you were faithful in all I gave you to bear. Share my joy."

He then walked over to the two ladies and spoke words of blessing and encouragement to them in English. After that, he held out his hands toward the teenagers and pronounced a blessing upon them.

He came back to Maurice and me and told us both, "In this life, you cannot know all things. Some happenings will remain a mystery to you. When you are with me one day, then you will be able to see completely how your actions were able to help me in my plans. Until then, you must trust me and acknowledge me in all your ways."

Then he said, "Daniel, please come with me to the side so we may speak apart from the rest."

I walked with him several feet to the left side of the stage, and he stopped and turned toward me.

"Daniel," he said, "We have not spoken about your life on Earth before you came to me."

"Lord, I am so ashamed that I was a major player in the greatest deception ever on Earth. I will have caused more damage through my pride and ambition than the Apostle Paul or Adolf Hitler or any of the communist tyrants like Stalin or Mao. I fear that millions, perhaps even billions, of people will be killed by the Perfects. And I helped by finding ways to create more of them, and I pushed their acceptance all around the world. I wish there were some way to make up for that, but I do not see how. The deaths of those who have been and will be killed are on me. If not for understanding your grace, I would be overwhelmed at the magnitude of the sufferings due to my blind devotion to humanism as opposed to your will."

He looked at me with warmth and affectionately touched my arm as he said, "Truly, what you and your organization did was a great evil. But since you repented publicly and then came to me to embrace the 'exchanged life,' you are completely forgiven. On the other hand, José Caliente initiated this great evil and continues to cause even more. His judgment at the Great White Throne will be severe."

He continued, "I need to tell you more about the Perfects as you called them. Because of the way the women were impregnated, they were not born as actual human beings. The saddest part is that they do not have the spirit, the living breath, in them as the other humans do. Therefore, even though they look and act like humans, they are not truly human. Because of that, none of them can be transformed into children of God through their trust in me and walk of obedience. That is why creating them was so incredibly and monstrously evil."

I obviously had a look of shock upon my face as he said further, "Do not blame yourself for these things. If you had not worked with José Caliente, then anyone of a number of other people would have come forward."

"Lord, I am so horrified. I don't know what to say. Will the Perfects succeed in killing off billions of humans? Who will be able to stop them?"

"Daniel, our Father has already made provisions for dealing with them. Even though you felt that their DNA was perfect, it has allowed them to be susceptible to certain kinds of diseases that are relatively unknown. Within the next few years, this disease will reach global pandemic proportions, and all of them will die of this disease, except for a few who will be isolated and protected. This coming judgment is indeed a horrible thing, but it must be done.

"Now I must return to the throne, although I have been there all along because all of Heaven is my throne. And while the door is open into Ontario, this entire world is part of my throne. Be encouraged, Daniel. There is much ahead for you and Maurice. You will face a great deal of persecution, but I will cause each of you to be protected until your appointed day to come home to me."

He then pulled me close for a hug. Even kissed me on the cheek, then he turned and walked back through the archway, continuing into the flowers. Leahu bid his friends farewell. As they expressed their affection for him, he again to glow brighter. Addressing Maniho fondly at the last, he walked through the opening, following his Lord. The Anakelani went back to inside the opening as before. The bright light appeared again and sealed the doorway shut. We were sitting in the square again, but now the suns were setting outside the city walls.

That night we bid each Kamiki we had known farewell, not knowing what would happen when the Anakela came in the morning. We then went to Maniho's study to talk extensively with him. We saw that his skin had started showing a faint glowing. He suggested we try to sleep to be ready for the visit. We hugged him farewell with tears.

I motioned for the others to leave first, and then I gave him my own special farewell with deep feelings.

"Maniho, you have been my one faithful friend through all of this. It is hard to tell you good bye. I have saved your life more than once, and you by your advice have saved mine many times. I will miss you very much, much more than I know how to say."

Maniho answered, "I treasure you as a dear friend as well. I had not known that someone such as you could be so precious to me. I shared your emotions and concerns more than any other Kamiki. I came to feel it with you. You have my greatest love and honor, Daniel Wayne Davidson."

He hugged me with the Kamiki hug and looked deeply into my eyes with a very warm smile. I saw love and respect in his smile and tears. And he saw the same in mine. I pulled him to me and held him close, then I turned and walked to the door. Looking back, I nodded farewell.

After he smiled and returned the nod, I went to my room and prepared for bed.

That night Aimee and I held each other close. We slept heavily that night, enveloped in feelings of peace that we had not known for a long time.

Chapter 22: The Promised Land

We awoke when the trumpets announced the dawn. Then a light appeared in our room. Aimee and I grabbed for robes and got out of bed. An Anakela materialized before us as if stepping through a door and quickly shutting it.

The bright figure addressed us in English, "I have been sent to take you to the appointed place. Bring all of your loved ones here as soon as you can, so I can tell you all how to prepare. I await here."

Aimee and I got dressed quickly and went to round up the others. Maurice and I also brought the best of the weapons, the healing robots, and the lifter. We assembled back in the room after final quick words to Kamiki friends along the way.

Speaking for the group, I announced to the Anakela, "We are ready."

The figure said, "I must tell you how you will return to Earth. Then you may ask me what Ahueha has told me of your final mission. You will travel through a portal to a location in Israel. You will not need weapons. You may take the healing robots and electronic devices, but the lifter and energy generator must remain here to keep it out of evil hands. Each of you may also take along one suitcase and no more."

"A Messianic Hebrew who speaks Hebrew waits for you there now. Ahueha showed him the place in a dream. He expects friends of God who speak English to arrive soon. He will carry you by van back to his rural home between Bethlehem and Jerusalem. There you will live and help around his property until the time of your next special work which will last for a season under great persecution but with much success. Also, you will be protected during that time. Be faithful and strong in the Lord, and all this will happen as I have told you."

The Anakela then moved to a corner of the room to wait, so I turned to the others and asked them to choose what to take and return to this place. As Maurice and I started selecting what we would put in our suitcases, we smiled lovingly at our wives who struggled to figure out what to leave. I included Grandpa Mike's Bible, one of my two electronic wallets, and some small keepsakes from Ontario.

Then Maurice asked the Anakela when we returned back there, "What will be our special work? We would like to prepare for it."

"Your work does not require any further preparation on your part. Ahueha knows but does not reveal it now. He will provide details as you need them."

Then I asked him, "Who is this man we go to meet?"

"His name is Jonathan Ben Samuel. He is a mighty man of prayer who hears God, and God hears him. You may trust him freely without reservation."

Looking at the others, I asked them, "Do any of you have questions?"

My son, Tim, asked, "What of us teenagers? And Maurice's children now away from home? What life will we have?"

"You here will marry in Israel and help your fathers and mothers in their special work. If you stay with them, you will have peace. If not, you will suffer and die at the hands of the new race and their supporters. Those not here must join you in Israel or suffer as I have said."

We had no further questions, and so the Anakela went to the center of the room and beckoned us to stand with him there. He waved his hand, and a door opened in space to reveal a dark place on the other side. The light from our room shown into the other side.

He motioned for us to pass through. We walked to the other side as he stayed on the side of Ontario. He stood at the door with his hands outstretched toward us and said, "Prosper well, friends of God. He blesses you. Go in his peace." Then the opening shrank quickly, and the light disappeared with it.

We were in a cave of some type, arriving during the night. We heard a sound just around the corner about 50 feet away. A man was whispering Hebrew exclamations, perhaps praises to God. He must have heard our arrival, because he turned on a flashlight. He was near the outside opening. He saw us and came timidly over to us and said in English, "Shalom, friends of God."

Maurice answered, "Hello, and peace be with you, friend of God."

I asked him, "What is your name?"

"I am Jonathan Ben Samuel. What are your names?"

Maurice told him, "We are the Davidsons and the Monterres. An angel said you would meet us."

Jonathan nodded and said, "Yes, God has told me by an angel in a vision. How may I help you?"

I informed him, "We were told we would live with you for some time. We will help around your place as we are able until the Lord reveals a new special work for us."

Excitedly, he exclaimed, "Of course! God is so wise! He sends you when I need seasonal help around my small farm. No Jew will help this Christian now. So, we will help each other! Bring your things and come with me to meet my wife and three children. You are welcome to stay with us as long as you like. Also, it is almost time for the evening meal. May God's blessings be upon you!"

Maurice and I both smiled and said, "May God's blessings also be upon you!"

Then I added, "We haven't had breakfast, and here we are having supper!"

We took our family's hands and followed him out of the cave. We loaded everything into his van and situated ourselves in the seats. It was a rather nice van, which indicated to me that God had been taking diligent care of Jonathan.

At his spacious home, we settled in and began to enjoy their hospitality. This lasted for several weeks, which enabled us to take care of Jonathan's expansive garden that he said he felt the Lord told him to set up. We all ate mostly fresh foods from the garden, which was improving our health dramatically.

On one morning after that, Maurice shared with us at breakfast that he had had a dream telling us to meet a certain woman who was over 100 years old. He said she was born in Israel to a Jewish family, and later she and they came to know Christ and became Messianic Jews themselves.

Jonathan became excited, saying that he knew who she was. He always knew there was something special about her, but he never could figure out what it was. He said he would introduce us to her, and then maybe he could finally find out what her role is in God's future plans.

Jonathan made the contact and set up our appointment with her. It turned out that she was in a lovely home because her parents had been very blessed of the Lord, and so was she. Maurice and I took our wives with us. When we arrived at the home and knocked on the door, a maid came and answered the door and showed us into where this woman was. She rose to meet us and seemed to be in fairly good health. She warmly hugged each of us and then motioned for us to take seats. We were sitting in comfortable couches arranged in a square. She sat in an easy chair at one corner of the square.

She then introduced herself in English, saying, "My name is Miriam Kaplan. Jonathan has already told me the rest of your names." She then proceeded to address each of us, correctly guessing each of our names.

Then she went on, "Jonathan tells me that you had a dream about me, and he shared the details of the dream. He also told me some of the things that you said happened to you in the home world of the Angels. I must admit this is all extremely hard to believe, but now that I see you, I can tell that you are speaking the truth. I also had a dream last night about this first meeting, which confirmed to me that what you experienced did indeed happen. Nevertheless, it is an incredible tale."

"Since the Lord revealed to you in a dream that I am a 'special woman,' I feel I should tell you more about me. Only my maid and three remarkably close Messianic Jewish friends know what I am about to share with you. I believe I can trust you with this knowledge if you swear to share it with no one else. And I do mean no one else outside of this room."

Maurice answered for us, "Since I was the one who had the dream, I am very anxious to hear more about you. And you can be assured that none of us will say anything about what you intend to share outside of this group. We will also be careful that when we discuss it among ourselves later that we will ensure there is no way anyone could be hearing us. We have tools to ensure complete privacy."

"Very well. Our Lord Yeshua has revealed to me in recent years certain things about my life. I have served him faithfully for over 60 years now. However, I have had to do so sometimes anonymously because of what the Lord has been showing me. You see, the end times with the seven-year tribulation in Revelation, the last book of the Holy Bible, cannot begin until the Lord has taken me home."

Well, that certainly got our attention. She continued on, "I was the first Jewish child to be born in this land immediately after your President Truman signed the 1948 proclamation reinstating Israel as the homeland of the Jewish people. This created a mystical union between the nation and me. However, I did not realize it until the Lord revealed it to me right before Israel and I reached 100 years old. As you can see, that means I am 107 years old now. He also told me not to share this with anyone other than a few people that he designates. If anyone knew of this, then there would be a massive effort to assassinate me so that Israel could undergo horrible persecution in order to wipe this nation off the world map."

At this point, I could not help but ask her, "This is almost as amazing as what our families have experienced on Ontario, the home world of young angels. To me the most obvious question then is to ask how long you think you will live."

She replied, "It says in Genesis 6:3 that God had decided that humans would from then on live no longer than 120 years. The Lord has told me that right before I turn 120 years old that it will be time for me to go home to heaven. Although religious experts disagree on the timing of the rapture of the saints, the Lord has revealed to me that I will be included with them in the Rapture right before the tribulation period. The Rapture will cause the hundreds of millions of people who have the Holy Spirit to be taken out from the Earth. That singular event will take away the great power source of the kingdom of Heaven and allow Satan to run amok. The Holy Spirit will come to inhabit those who believe in Christ after the Rapture, but their initial numbers will be low at the outset."

Maurice said, "What about the Scripture that says no one knows the day and hour for Jesus' return, or when the rapture will occur?"

She explained, "Yes, not the day and the hour. Yeshua told us to know the seasons and get ready. Don't you feel we are in the season that is awfully close to the end?"

Maurice thought for a moment and answered, "Yes, I do believe it. I don't see how it can be any other way. All of the technology is in place, and the population levels are adequate to staff the end time armies. I don't see how the Lord will wait beyond just a few more decades, if that."

After Maurice's comment she sat back for a moment, seemingly lost in thought. Then she said, "There is a man who lives nearby that I trust as a New Covenant prophet. He has predicted many things very accurately in recent years. He told me that I would be meeting some people who would be major players in the end-time activities. One would be a man who had long stood for God's truth. The other would be a man who caused great evil and then repented of it, after which he acknowledged Yeshua as his Lord and Savior. He would come to see me this week with the other man to find out what they should do. Maurice and Daniel, you are obviously those two men. He said when I met you that I should let him know so that he might tell you what God has shown him about your future. Do you mind if we try to meet here together again tomorrow night?"

We and our wives said that we would certainly be interested in meeting with him. We talked with her for a while longer and then went back to get a good night's rest. The next morning her servant called and told us what time to be back at her house to meet with the prophet. She also told us that Miriam wanted to treat us to an exceptionally fine dinner before we talked in detail with the prophet.

Jonathan went with us the next night, and a jubilant man met us just outside her front door.

"I have longed to meet you ever since the Lord told me about you. An angel appeared before me in the night around two weeks ago and shared with me things that I should tell you. I believe you would be glad to know what God has planned for you."

He introduced himself as Elisha Levine, and we all shook hands and went inside to meet Miriam in the dining room. She had a lavish dinner prepared for us, including beef and chicken with many vegetable dishes and authentic Hebrew desserts. We talked about the Lord, what was happening in Israel and in the world, and we even shared a few jokes. It was good to share laughter like that. Afterwards, we met in the same study as on the previous night.

After we were settled, Maurice asked Elisha to share with us what he had heard the angel say. He began, "He told me a few things about you and then said that you will from now on take on new names instead of your birth names, and you must grow beards and wear hats. Daniel will become David, which means Beloved. Maurice will become Joseph, which means "he will add" or "increase." You must also change your middle and last names, and I trust these will come to you in dreams. Miriam and I can help you with getting the legitimate papers and accounts set up for your new names. Based upon what the angel told me, I have also contacted some Messianic Jewish friends who have a growing business that needs to establish a scientific research team. If you wish to work for them, then I can set up the meeting for you to discuss what your business relationship would be. I understand they already have a remarkably well-equipped research laboratory.

At that point, I offered, "This sounds like a wonderful opportunity, and I believe that both Maurice and I would be glad to talk with them." Maurice nodded in agreement.

The prophet continued, "Good! I will set up that meeting as soon as possible. The Lord also told me that on evenings and the weekends, you would also be working in Christian ministry under the power and anointing of apostles, and he asked me to work with you as a team. If it is acceptable to you, I will include you in the meetings and classes that I have already established. I have started reaching greater numbers of people as time goes on. The Lord has said that the two of you will eventually take the lead, and that I would be a strong prophetic support. We will be working in apostolic and prophetic anointings together. We will be able to do a few miracles, signs, and wonders in the beginning. Our capabilities as a team will grow as you mature into this type of ministry."

Maurice then interjected, "Prophet, this is incredible news. I suppose I am wondering how as this ministry grows that we can keep secret who we are. And will we draw so much attention that we will become so famous that it will create problems for us and our families?"

He laughed. "I wondered about that myself. I asked the Lord how we can keep you protected when word gets out that we are performing miracles, signs, and wonders that are verifiable and cannot be ignored. We know as word gets out that people will start flocking to us for the displays of power in Messiah's authority. It could become, as you say, a circus."

"The Lord assured me that the media of the world will become so corrupt that it will intentionally overlook anything that shows that there is a God and that he is active. Anything that honors our Yeshua will cause them to stay away in order to keep the word from getting out through public channels. However, word about God working with us will still get out, and people from many countries will come seeking a touch from God. In a few years, we will also set up conferences and seminars for other Christian leaders to be able to grow in the things that we are accomplishing. He also said that we would be able to do this successfully until the Rapture of the Saints. I have written all of this down, and I can share it with you soon."

"I need to add that there will be a great deal of persecution from some places, especially within traditional religious organizations. They will do all they can to shut us down, but if we trust the Lord to guide us, he will always cause us to be victorious over them. We will enjoy watching this completely frustrate them, but they will not be able to do anything about it. Furthermore, God will protect us from interference by public officials. When our religious enemies try to get them involved, they will insist that these are religious affairs that are none of their business."

We discussed all of these things for about another hour, and then we needed to return to our homes to rest for the night. Miriam also offered that she had known the prophet for a long time and encouraged us to trust him about everything that he was sharing with us. Maurice and I said that we and our wives would be discussing this further, but we saw no reasons not to continue on with this revealed plan.

Tomorrow would see the beginning of the rest of our lives. And we were all overjoyed and overwhelmed with the opportunities before us.

About the Author

Malcolm Wayne Puckett was born and raised in the beautiful Bluegrass region of central Kentucky. He moved to central Georgia in his 30's and retired as a supervisor-manager from Robins Air Force Base, having been in facility engineering, community planning, and quality improvement. His home is now with his wife just south of Jacksonville, Florida. He earned a B.S. in electrical engineering, a Master's in religious education, and a Ph.D. in engineering management. He achieved many academic and professional awards during his education and career. As a committed Christian who loves science fiction, he especially enjoys books written from a Biblical world-view. Also, his personal walk through psychological issues has made him sensitive to the struggles we all face in our daily lives, which is reflected in the struggles of the main character in this book.

www.ingramcontent.com/pod-product-compliance
Lightning Source LLC
Chambersburg PA
CBHW071911220626
47052CB00002B/310